The Treasure of Santa Maria

To his dying day, Monte Crawford never understood why he had saved Grover Lang's life. It was one of those unfathomable things – since it certainly wasn't in his nature to help others.

Whatever the reasons, Crawford's uncharacteristic act of kindness leads to all kinds of unforeseen consequences: blood, mayhem and death, as the perilous journey to the legendary treasure of Santa Maria begins. . . .

By the same author

Gunsmoke in Vegas
Catfoot

The Treasure of Santa Maria

J. William Allen

A Black Horse Western

ROBERT HALE · LONDON

ISBN 978-0-7090-8935-3

Robert Hale Limited
Clerkenwell House
Clerkenwell Green
London EC1R 0HT

www.halebooks.com

For a princess: Chardonnay Truin

Typeset by
Derek Doyle & Associates, Shaw Heath
Printed and bound in Great Britain by
CPI Antony Rowe, Chippenham and Eastbourne

1

'Joe! Joe!'

He turned at the shout. Joe wasn't his name but he had been using Joe Stockton as an alias for some time so there was every chance the yell was to attract his attention. Especially out here in a semi-wilderness with no other soul in sight.

There was a man waving from the long grass. Monte Crawford pulled the wagon to a halt and jammed on the brake.

The man was standing proud of the vegetation and looked agitated. There had to be some problem. The way the fellow was waving his arms it looked like a life-or-death problem.

'What is it?' Crawford called back as the man started heading towards him.

Crawford waited for a moment, fingering his pockmarked cheek. But then the man stopped and just stood there, beckoning him.

Nonplussed, Crawford dropped down from the wagon and started wading through the grass. He was wary. He had never made a legal dollar in his life, but he had never stooped to bushwhacking. However, that didn't mean that others didn't, so he undid his jacket, making sure that his gun was accessible, and proceeded cautiously. At first he didn't recognize the fellow, who was dressed in civilian clothes. But as they approached each other, he could identify him as Corporal Stevens.

'What gives?' he asked as they came face to face. 'And why are you out of uniform?'

'They're on to us,' Stevens said. 'That's why I've dumped my uniform. You're lucky I've met you like this, otherwise you'd have rode right into the hornet's nest.'

'How much of a hornet's nest?'

The man looked back along the trail. 'It's in the hands of the provost marshal. You know what that means if his boys catch us?'

'Remind me.'

'Given the emergency regulations, a firing squad.'

Crawford mouthed a 'Jesus' and made his own inspection of the soldier's back trail.

'Can't stay here jawing,' Stevens said. 'The provost marshal is the meanest bastard who ever put on a uniform. I tell you, he won't give up on either of us. And then it's the firing squad.'

6

'But I'm a civilian. I can't be executed like that.'

'Won't make no never-mind to him. Extreme times call for extreme action. Your best bet is to get the hell out of here. Like I'm doing.' He resumed his race through the grass, shouting, 'Best of luck, pal,' over his shoulder.

Back at the wagon Crawford pondered on the situation. For a start, the provost marshal would be looking for a wagon, so his first task was to dump it. He gigged the horses and turned the wagon off the trail opposite to the way in which Stevens had gone, the animals making heavy going through the grass. Eventually he topped a rise and, checking that the wagon wouldn't be seen in the dip beyond the ridge, he pulled in.

His newly imposed priority was to put as many miles as he could between himself and the camp in the quickest time, and shank's pony was not the best means of locomotion. He dropped down and studied the horses, figuring how he could use one. There were two problems. He didn't know whether either had ever been used as a saddle horse; worse, he would have to ride it bareback. He checked each in turn, patting its back and figuring which was the less skittish. When he had chosen the one he deemed the more docile he fashioned the ribbons into makeshift reins which he fixed to the bridle. He scatted the other horse.

Without stirrups there would be difficulty

mounting the horse. But at least it was not so high as a standard saddle horse and, after varied attempts in which he and animal completed several awkward circles, he managed to get astride it.

To make as much distance as he could, he rode throughout the rest of the day ignoring settlements along the way. It was dark when the exhausted man and horse passed a sign heralding the township of Middleton. Money being no problem as he had the takings from his last transaction – he booked into a hotel.

Giving up his attempt to sleep for the moment, he went to the window and looked the street over. When he saw there were no soldiers he lit a cigarette.

Some men don a uniform because the impetus of events make it difficult to avoid joining the ranks. Not natural men of action, they find themselves under a variety of pressures. A militaristic father might expect a son to defend the honour of the South. Or your pals might call you coward if you didn't take the oath with them. Others enlist on principle. They have a cause to fight for.

Although he was not yet aware of it, it was principle that would cause Monte Crawford to join: the mundane principle of saving his neck.

He stubbed out the cigarette, returned to the bed and watched the reflections from the street flickering in the ceiling.

A man of his outlook saw every set of circumstances as an opportunity. Come the outbreak of hostilities he had had no more intention of joining the army than he had of going to church on Sundays. But the war presented him with a set of circumstances. Notably he had observed that prices of goods – from luxuries to basics – had gone through the roof. Other folk griped, but not he. He kept watch on prices, noted that prices varied from locality to locality, and he purchased small surpluses from farmers, which he then sold in some town where he knew prices were higher. But, as the war progressed, farmers fell into the habit of hanging on to every grain they could. Then he had competition from the army who began commandeering supplies from civilians. Pickings and surpluses became very difficult to come by.

His own dealings with the army began in a small way. At the beginning of the war, the Confederate Army had set up a base just out of town. At first, it served as temporary quarters for units on their way to the front. Crawford worked his way in, offering to take horses that, with broken limbs, ill or simply exhausted, were no longer serviceable. These he took and sold to civilians as meat. This was reasonably profitable until the army realized it could eat its own horses.

But by '65 the Confederacy was losing its war and

the local camp became a fallback point, its numbers increasing with soldiers who had retreated. By this time the army bureaucrats had become more efficient at organizing supplies and the camp had become the regional focus for large amounts of incoming provisions.

So vast was the quantity that he figured they wouldn't miss a wagon here and there. His track record of dealing with the army gave him a twofold advantage. Not only had he become a well-known figure in the camp, and so his presence wouldn't be seen as suspicious, but he had also become familiar with many army personnel. Particularly he knew those with whom he could strike informal deals.

Thus it was, via his inside man in the shape of a Corporal Stevens, that he began another profitable operation, one of siphoning off army supplies which he sold at top dollar to merchants. He was wise enough to ensure that transactions were always done some distance away from the camp and with merchants who would ask no questions.

He could have seen the war out this way, had it not been for his being greedy, which caused the chief procurement officer to become suspicious and set up an investigation.

Crawford had known nothing of the case against him – or how serious its consequences could be for him – until that afternoon when he had heard the shout coming from the long grass at the side of the trail along which he was travelling after a delivery.

And now all hell could break loose.

Early next day he bought a change of clothing and headed for the livery stable with the intention of buying a regular saddle horse. Along the boardwalk the talk amongst the townsfolk was all about the war. Although he aimed to get on his way as soon as possible he didn't feel any urgency, getting some comfort from the notion that the army wouldn't know where he was. As far as they knew he could have fled to any point on the compass. Of course they would put some effort into the chase, he figured, but then they would give up. After all, they did have the more important matter of a war on their hands. Moreover, a war that wasn't going too well for them.

It was in this relatively unguarded frame of mind that he made his way through the shoppers.

That was until he saw two grey uniforms on the other side of the street. He took cover in a doorway and watched. The purposive stride of one and the deferential demeanour of the one trailing behind suggested an officer and aide. From his hidden vantage point he studied the officer. Didn't recognize him. But there was something familiar in the features of the second. He was pretty sure he'd seen him in the camp. In that case the man would know Crawford.

11

His heart began to thump. He didn't know the provost marshal – so the officer wouldn't recognize him – but the ranker he was pulling along with him was likely to identify Crawford. He had to act on the assumption that these two army men were after him. His notion was given weight when they entered the law office. On such a mission it would be automatic, he reckoned, that they would seek the assistance of civilian lawmen.

He waited until the door was closed behind them, and then hot-footed to the livery stable.

It took him some time to get used to the gait of the new animal but eventually he was into its rhythm. And having a saddle under him was better than riding bareback. But having a sore backside was the least of his troubles as he repeatedly cussed himself for his complacency. He'd been too complacent when going around town. In fact he'd been too complacent in showing his face in a town at all.

He had no idea where he was headed. Now only one thought gripped his brain: to get as far from Middleton as possible.

2

It was around noon when he reined in. Way ahead, faint in the distance, a sound like thunder. Rain on the way? He nudged his mount back to a gallop and was pondering on how a change in weather would affect his situation, when he pulled in again. The sound had become much louder, more distinct – and it wasn't thunder. It was a mixture of artillery and small arms fire. He was headed plumb into a war theatre.

He stood high in the stirrups and squinted into the distance. He couldn't see anyone or detect smoke so he couldn't locate the action with the result that he didn't know whether he should turn west or east to avoid the conflict. But the decision became academic for him when he glanced back. There were two dots on the horizon.

Two riders on his back trail! He had to act on the assumption they were his pursuers.

That was enough for him to spur his horse to its limit.

A mile on he spotted soldiers ahead, a straggly ribbon of Union blue stretching across the easterly horizon. Spasms of gunfire crackled, interspersed with the thunderclap of artillery. He reined in again. The Northerners were advancing. That meant they would have the upper hand.

The trail ahead rose and he nudged the horse towards it to give him a better vantage point. To the west he could make out retreating grey figures. A glance back showed him that not only did he still have company on the trail, but they had made some leeway. With the reduced distance between them he could make out that they wore grey uniforms, making it a sure bet they were the two who were set to stand him before a firing squad.

Riding straight ahead would take him between the two forces. Turning east could put him under fire with the retreating infantry. What to do? He wheeled the horse and cut off the trail at a right angle and rode west. Keeping his distance from the Federal troops and riding parallel to the line would be enough, he reckoned, to keep him out danger. As a civilian he would be unlikely to be a specific target of the opposing soldiers. Moreover, the grey-clad soldiers to his rear would be foolhardy to follow him so close to what was probably now enemy-held territory.

14

All went well until he heard a ghostly whistle and the ground close to him exploded. With a terrified whinny the horse reared, throwing its rider to the grass. Must have been a shell from the retreating Confederates. He staggered to his feet but all he could see of his horse was a fast-receding rump. He looked back. His pursuers had been persistent and had cut across the sward in parallel. He broke into a run northwards, noting that the tail end of the Federals was now to his west.

Would his pursuers dare to follow him?

As he ran he kept looking back. The land rose and fell so that sometimes he saw them, other times they were out of sight. Breathing heavily, he fell against a tree. What should he do? It looked like they weren't giving up on him. If they maintained their pursuit with the vigour they had hereto shown, being on horseback it wouldn't be long before they caught him.

He started to run again. How long he plunged through the grass, up and down inclines, he didn't know. One thing he did know – he was becoming exhausted and wouldn't be able to keep up the pace much longer.

He topped a rise and rolled down into the hollow, fetching up on his back, his lungs grasping for air. It was then that he saw he wasn't alone in the dip. Nearby lay the crumpled body of a Confederate. He crawled over to the form. It was a young man with a bloody hole in the side of his head.

'As they say, pal, the war for you is over.'

He wormed his way up the ridge and peered cautiously over the rim. He couldn't see his pursuers but that didn't mean they weren't out there somewhere.

Keeping to a crouch he scrabbled back down and made to continue along the bed of the hollow; then he stopped and looked back at the corpse. His pursers were looking for a civilian and the man was about his size.

Maybe. . . .

He didn't have to think on the matter much longer. Whatever the downside of wearing a uniform it was better than being dressed in clothes recognizable by those close on his heels, still chasing him and likely to turn up at any time. He returned and began stripping the body. When he'd finished the exchange of clothes, he dragged the unfortunate's remains and heaved them under some scrub. They weren't completely hidden but in such a position might not arouse the interest of a casual observer.

Minutes later he was journeying across the terrain. Disguised, he no longer felt the need to run and took the opportunity to walk in an easy manner and recapture his breath.

Suddenly his random looks back suggested that

his pursuers, as if by magic, had disappeared. He took cover behind a tree and studied his back trail more keenly. No sign. The fighting was now a faint noise in the distance and constant scouring of his surroundings suggested he had lost his pursuers. Maybe; but he wouldn't lay a price on it. But it was of declining concern. Even if they did spot him from afar, the grey uniform he now wore should not attract their attention.

Had they merely lost sight of him? For whatever reason, thankfully he seemed to have the world to himself.

But when he turned in preparation to proceed he could see why his pursuers had chosen this moment to make themselves scarce. He could make out a body of soldiers on the skyline. He squinted and could see it was a unit of Northern infantry escorting Confederate prisoners. He didn't take long to reach a decision and he turned in their direction.

When they were nearer and could clearly see him, he dropped to the ground, feigning a stumble. He grabbed handfuls of dirt and worked the stuff into his features. He spat on his hands and rubbed the dirt, streaking and darkening it as though the mess had been compounded by sweat. After he had mussed up his hair even more, he hauled himself to his feet and continued.

He raised his hands as high as he could and was

taken into custody with no show of animosity. The way he saw it, the likely deprivations of some prison camp would be preferable to a firing squad.

3

The sound of distant water permeated his stupefied brain. What was it? Couldn't be rain. Maybe a river.

Captain Lang could not make sense of things any more. Sweats came and went with regularity. When his brain had still been working, just before he was captured, he'd reckoned he was developing some kind of fever with all the fatigue that went with it.

It was late afternoon and the sad-looking column of Confederate prisoners was trudging two abreast towards St Louis. Rumour had it they were headed for some federal military prison at a place called Alton. They were accompanied by only a handful of armed men in blue. No one wanted to escape; the fight was gone from all of the Southerners.

Each step was increased torment for Lang. He had become aware of muscles in his legs and body that he never knew he had. He forced up his head for a moment, long enough for his weary eyes to make out that they were approaching a bridge. The sound of water of which he had become aware was coming from beneath it.

The bridge was a sorry-looking specimen, having been hit by a shell during recent action. An advance party of their captors had checked it out. The thing was still serviceable but rickety, with some of its railing gone.

'Keep to the left side,' someone bellowed. 'Near the rail.'

As the prisoners' boots hit the wooden planking with a weird echoing sound, Lang's head began to spin. The sweats were back with a vengeance and he was fast losing strength. He didn't know how much further he could go. Then consciousness began draining fast. He swayed one way, then the other. His last thought was to grab the rail, but he tottered uncontrollably in the opposite direction and pitched over the unprotected side.

Prisoners shouted.

'What's happening there?' some officer hollered.

'Old feller, Sarge,' a corporal replied. 'Fatigued, lost his footing. Just fell.'

The officer walked tentatively to the exposed edge and looked down. He could make out a form swirling in the current below. 'Nobody'll miss him. Keep it moving. We got a schedule to meet.'

Monte Crawford broke ranks and ran to the edge. He took one look at the figure rolling uncontrollably downstream and, without a thought, he simply dived in. Later he was to ask himself why would he have done such a thing. He couldn't come up with a satisfactory answer because it had never been his nature to help anybody. The only thing he could put it down to was the fact that he had been doing nothing but march for two days and needed some kind of activity, anything to break the monotony.

He hit the water awkwardly but, the drop being only a short distance, it didn't trouble him unduly and, on coming to the surface, he struck out.

Back on the bridge the corporal pointed downwards. 'What do we do, Sarge?' he wanted to know. 'Leave 'em?'

'No.' The officer pointed to the nearest soldiers. 'You two, get down there and bring 'em back. Mislaying one might be acceptable but these guys have been counted and I ain't reporting I've lost two of the critters without due cause.'

With the current behind him Crawford made good headway and soon caught up with the drifting figure. The cold water had brought Lang somewhat to his senses but his weak flailing was without effect. The younger man grabbed his collar and struck against the current making for the side. But the force of water threw him against a partially submerged rock and he caught his head.

Despite the thump he eventually made the edge.

Now exhausted himself, he hauled the form on to the bank and dropped on to his back. The two panting figures remained in that position until they were joined by the pair of soldiers.

'How is he?' one asked.

'Reckon he'll make it,' Crawford gasped, without opening his eyes.

'Nasty gash you got there,' the other observed.

Crawford didn't reply or investigate the wound, content just to lie there, pulling in air.

'OK,' a soldier said, 'keep close to us while we get the old feller topside.'

Back on the bridge the sergeant gave orders for Lang to be put on to a wagon.

He looked at the bleeding Crawford, drenched and rocking unsteadily. 'You and he buddies or som'at?'

The young man managed to get out the words 'No, sir,' before collapsing.

The sergeant looked down at the crumpled figure and shook his head. 'Put him on the wagon with the other one. We'll get the doc to look them over when we bivouac tonight.'

Shortly, when Crawford came to, he was shivering and aware he was bouncing on the planking of some wagon. Space had been made to lay the two men in between bags and other varied supplies. Jeez, his head was thumping. He explored the source of the pain and examined the blood on his fingertips. Before dropping his head back he glanced at the man beside him.

Why the hell had he exerted himself to help a complete stranger? And what had he got for his trouble? A thorough soaking and crack on the skull.

Well, if nothing else he had got himself a free ride.

The evening bivouac was a motley sprawl dotted with campfires. Crawford rose from the pallet in the temporary sick bay. His headache had gone and he felt hungry.

'Folks tell me it was you who fetched me out of the drink,' the man beside him said.

Crawford shrugged. 'If they say so.'

The man offered a weakly raised hand. 'Captain Lang, that is Grover Lang, formerly of the Missouri Fifth Infantry, at your service, sir.'

The other squinted into the darkness in search of a clue to the whereabouts of eats. 'Happy to make your acquaintance, Captain.' He allowed his own hand to be briefly shaken. 'Monte Crawford, formerly of the . . . the . . . oh, take your pick.'

'Well, I'm in your debt, Mr Crawford.'

'And I'm told you're on the mend,' the younger man said, fingering the dressing on his own wound. 'Your fever's broke.'

With that he disappeared into the night in search of food.

*

A week later the contingent found themselves trudging along the banks of the Missouri on their way to St Louis. As they neared the city they passed the dockyards where Federal gunboats were under construction.

Grover Lang, now reasonably restored and able to walk, paused to look at the work.

'Hey, you, keep moving,' a uniformed man shouted.

Lang saluted histrionically before resuming walking. 'Yes, sir.'

'And keep your eyes ahead.'

'Yes, sir.'

The soldier kept in step with him. 'And that's why you Rebs are gonna lose the war. As you can see, we got what it takes to do it – the ships and guns.'

'No doubt.'

The soldier appraised the prisoner. He was tall and had a demeanour that in other circumstances might have been deemed aristocratic.

'You some kind of gentleman?'

'That is the prerogative of others to say.'

'Southern gentleman crap,' the soldier scoffed and sniffed his disgruntlement. 'I hate Southerners. You got this idea that you're something different, above the rest of America. That's what all this secession business is about. Rebels don't see

24

themselves as subject to American law. And you guys especially, you Southern gentlemen, stick in my craw. Looking down your noses at ordinary folk. All that social class stuff. This is America, we don't have social classes. We leave all that to the Europeans.'

Eventually the soldier was called away for other duties and Crawford fell in step beside Lang. 'Interesting conversation.'

'Neither a conversation or interesting.'

Once they had reached the prison and settled in Crawford and Lang saw little of each other, especially during the day. The place was massively overcrowded with more prisoners arriving each day. And when the major in charge of the establishment learned that Lang had some education, he was detailed to join the clerks handling the paperwork.

It was the same when he had joined up for the Confederacy. When it got through to the brass hats that he could not only read and write but had worked on the railroad before the war, he had been promoted and put in charge of a unit responsible for building or repairing bridges.

But the mechanics of bridges had been new to him. He was not an engineer. In his civilian times with the railroad he had been a surveyor exploring territory seeking to establish the best routes for laying track. He was not called on to use these skills in the army. But he learned enough to meet the demands made upon him, at least enough to pass muster and to give him an easy war. That was until his unit surrendered and he found himself a prisoner-of-war in a camp where it was dog eat dog.

For his part, Monte Crawford had seen the prison as nothing more than providing a safe haven. But then, as the pattern of his life had been thus far, he had recognized it as presenting him with a new set of opportunities. Forever on the *qui vive*, looking and listening, he had soon learned how the system worked and, by making friends in profitable places, had wormed his way into it. The result: before long the other prisoners had found him to be the man you turned to if you wanted anything, a scrap of extra food, a bit of tobacco.

It had gone well until he had been caught in possession of a stock of canned food and the officers knew it could only have been stolen from the stores. The finding had led to a search in which his large store of scrip and commodities had been unearthed. From then on his captors had kept him at work for all available hours – grave-digging in the burgeoning cemetery, unloading wagons and, as now, laundry detail.

'Stop talking, Reb!' The rasped command was accompanied by a sharp jab with a rifle butt between his shoulder blades. 'And scrub those clothes harder!'

4

That evening Crawford stared at his reddened hands, still stinging from their soaking in soda. 'What a life.'

'We are all used to better, my friend.'

He turned to check the speaker. It was Grover Lang.

'Hey, Grover. Not seen you for a spell.'

'They keep me busy pen-pushing.'

Crawford showed his hands. 'You're lucky. Sitting behind a desk you don't get mitts like this.'

'Look on the bright side. We're not being shot at each day – and we still have some luxuries.' He took out a drawstring bag. 'Here, my friend, have a smoke, help take your mind off things.'

'Where did you get that?' Crawford said.

'Bought it from you, didn't I? When you were the camp supplier.'

'Huh, that's all over.'

'Yes. I heard how the guards discovered your cache.'

'That cache helped keep me sane.'

'And helped you to be top of the heap.'

'Yeah. And now I'm the lowest of the low with the guards keeping an especial eye on me.

The men fiddled with the makings until a few minutes later they were relaxing with glowing cigarettes.

'For them to give you an office job you must be an educated man,' Crawford said. 'What did you do for a living before donning the grey?'

'Worked as a surveyor for the railroad.'

'Ah, a professional man. I thought so. A good position.'

'I got by. And you?'

'Not a trade like you. Bit of everything. Anything that would turn a dollar. But, like you, I got by.'

They smoked in silence until Lang killed his cigarette. 'We're not going to win this war,' he said, as he salvaged the remaining strands of tobacco from his finished cigarette. 'The odds have been stacked against us from the moment the first guns were fired at Fort Sumter. We only have one thing going for us: morale. Our guys are determined – they're fighting for a cause – while those in the Yankee ranks are only fighting because they've been told to. But they have the wherewithal. All we got is heart.'

Crawford didn't say anything; he couldn't care less who won. All he wanted was to get out of this damn place. Principles were for losers.

'Right from the start,' the older man continued, 'the best thing we could get out of the thing was a stalemate and a truce; a vain hope that those with intelligence would sue for peace, bring the mayhem to a close and we could get a few of our demands met. The idea that we could set up a separate state – as Texas once did – was a notion built on sand.'

After a while he stood up, walked a few paces and gazed out over the river. 'Look over there. It's night time but over in St Louis the place is like daylight.'

'Hadn't noticed.'

'They've got this newfangled gas lighting everywhere. The Confederacy can't fight an enemy that's got access to technology like that. It's like another world. On the way in, did you see the shipyards where the Federal gunboats are being constructed. Those Feds have got us beat on land and at sea.'

He returned and sat down again. 'Hear tell this place was originally built as a prison.'

'Didn't know that,' Crawford mouthed without much interest.

'Yeah, a place to hold common criminals.' He thought on it and added, 'We're criminals too.'

'Criminals?' Crawford's eyebrows had risen

slightly. He didn't like the word. 'How do you make that out?'

'We lost a war – and lived. That's criminal.'

Crawford's big chance came when smallpox broke out in the camp. At first there was panic. The prisoners rioted and were only brought to order with gunfire. Then cases were isolated. But when the number of those succumbing to the illness escalated, all victims – Reb and Union alike as the pox was no respecter of the difference between grey and blue – were shipped out to an island in the middle of the river.

One morning an officer addressed the prisoners – from a distance – asking if there was anyone amongst the throng who had already suffered from the disease. It was well known that anyone who had once survived the illness was unlikely to catch it again and therefore was ideal for tending to the sick. Two raised their hands. One was Crawford. He did not do so for altruistic reasons. He immediately realized the privileged position in which it could put him. It could give him the edge he had lost.

The two men were asked to step forward.

'Are you sure you've had the pox before?' the officer asked, still keeping at a distance. 'Because if you're lying you'll surely catch it and you only have to look at the lime pits to know what that means.'

Crawford pointed to the pockmarks on his face.

His misdemeanours were forgotten. Although he still worked long hours, he wasn't under close supervision and his life became easier for that. And it wasn't long before liquor – in the form of medical alcohol – became a profitable line for him. He was in business once more.

Weeks past and the guards' became so occupied with handling the large number of prisoners coming in each day that Crawford's new sideline was not noticed.

One day he and Lang were watching a new batch being herded into the compound.

The news from all the newcomers amounted to the same thing. The end was near.

'When this business is over, you going back to your trade?' Crawford asked.

'Maybe eventually,' the other said. 'But not directly.'

'So what are your plans?'

'Nothing precise. Just been kicking some ideas around is all.'

He didn't expand on what he meant by this until a few days later.

The day in question was a weird one. They awoke to a buzz going round the camp. Rumours that the South's surrender was imminent were intermixed with stories that it had already happened. But at lunchtime firm details came through. Lee had surrendered to Grant at some place called Appomattox.

Although it meant the war was lost those interns who'd had enough of the whole mess ran about whooping and hollering. Those who had been fighting for a cause sat glumly either alone or commiserating with buddies.

Crawford was standing at a wire fence looking across the river when Lang joined him. 'Some news, eh?' Lang said.

'Yeah.'

They shared a silence, each with his own thoughts.

'I been thinking,' the older man said eventually. 'You've been good to me.'

'I've told you to forget it.'

'Nevertheless, I was wondering if you and I might pal up for a spell. You know, now the war is over.'

Crawford said nothing so the other went on. 'See, I got this project in mind. I have a brother. Jim, younger than me. Good lad, hard worker. I would have liked him to come aboard but he cleared off at the outbreak of war. Last I heard he was in Mexico. The venture calls for three, or at least two, men. Well, as you and I have been pretty close for a spell, I thought of you.'

'So what is it?' Crawford said half-heartedly.

'It'd mean taking a chance. But it could mean big dollars.'

That gained the listener's attention so Lang continued. 'Yeah, could be a jackpot. On the other hand we might end up with a hill of beans.'

Crawford looked askance. 'OK, tell me more.'

'Loading up with the right kit and going out to the wide open spaces, breathing fresh air – and looking for gold.'

'Prospecting?' Crawford exclaimed. 'Hell, Grover, I thought you had a good idea for the moment. Jeez, prospecting? I ain't never heard of a prospector making it. Most I seen ain't got more than a pot to shit in.'

'There's truth in that, my friend. But hear me out. Fact is, there are three kinds of prospector. There's the type that hears of a strike and joins the rush. They're the ones you see with their ass hanging out of their pants. Sheep, losers down to a man – and they're the bulk of those involved. Those are the types that you're thinking of. The only ones who make anything out of a strike are the original finders – and the camp followers who sell supplies and mining paraphernalia to the punters. They make a good living, selling everything at top dollar.

'Then, there's another kind: the lone old-timers who spend their life roaming the wilderness, chipping away rock here, sieving water there. Over the years they build up some knowledge and, once in a blue moon, one of 'em will hit the jackpot. But it's rare.'

'If you're trying to entice me into joining you, you're not painting a very attractive picture, Captain.'

Lang smiled. 'Then there's the third type: the ones who already have the knowledge.'

'So what are you telling me?'

'I spent all my younger years covering the West, making maps for the railroad. In that capacity, I chipped away at rocks. It was my job to assess terrain for ease in laying down rail tracks. My bosses weren't in the ore business, so if I saw some potential for mining there was no requirement on me to tell them.'

'If you're not a prospector, how would you recognize potential?'

'In building up qualifications for the job I did quite a few years at college. One of our studies was called geology. The subject is getting more acceptable now but it was new then. It teaches you what is likely to be under the ground. The upshot is, twenty years of combining theory with the practical work in the field has given me a few ideas.'

'You telling me you know places where's there gold?'

Lang chuckled. 'No, but I can recognize locations, indeed know of some, where there is a good chance of there being some kind of precious metal. That's where the unpredictability comes in. So, the project will mean hard work and there'll be no guarantee. But with what I know the odds are good. The way I see the matter, it'll be like putting a wager on a horse based on inside information. If you know anything about the sport of kings, you will know such an action has no certainty. But repeated betting on inside information will put a guy ahead of the ordinary punter.'

There was a pause. Then Lang asked, 'Well? Fancy coming aboard?'

There was another pause, this time broken by Crawford. 'Have you ever been a salesman in your varied career?'

'No.'

'Well, you've sold me. Seeing I got no immediate plans.'

The older man chuckled, and they shook hands.

5

Using a piece of folded paper as a funnel, Lang carefully poured the dust into a drawstring bag, the yield for the day. He pulled the cords and tied a loose knot, then handed the bag to his comrade.

Crawford weighed the bag in his hand. 'And how much will this fetch?'

Lang shrugged. 'Depends on the quality. Maybe twenty dollars or more.'

'That's ten dollars each! Ten dollars for a day's work? Hell!'

'Look on the bright side. It's more than a guy can make working cattle.'

'Yeah. Just. But it ain't my idea of the high life, Captain.'

'We've been up here for three months. That's long enough for you to know there could be a lot more tomorrow. We've had our good days.'

'There you go with your "could-bes" and "tomorrows".'

36

'Everything in life has a chance element to it. The knack is to balance matters in your favour. That's what we've been doing. Give me credit. Not many hit gold on their first diggings. We did, albeit no great shakes thus far but it was my prior work and research that led to it.'

He reclaimed the bag, allowing Crawford to pat his arms in an attempt to bring some warmth into them. 'And this ain't the warmest place in God's Own Country, Grover. Montana – for hell's sake. Why Montana?'

Lang's last commission before the war had been with the North Pacific Railroad during the course of which he had cause to map large areas of Montana. His knowledge of rock formations and their chemistry had suggested to him where there was some probability of precious metal. Which was why, when they had been repatriated and demobilized, he had drawn on his savings to finance the two of them on the long trek to the North-West. And he had been right. It hadn't been long before he had followed clues to a source. Only trouble was, as Crawford had pointed out more than once, the pickings were not going to make them millionaires.

The younger man looked along the frosted valley and then threw a curt glance at the snow-topped mountains. Canada was hitting them with a harsh wind.

'What's wrong with California?' he went on.

'That's known for gold – and they got sun down there.'

'They got sun down there all right – and thousands of hopefuls who are making less than a peck of apples apiece.'

Crawford grunted. 'As I understand it, prospectors always stop fifteen feet shy of the mother lode.'

'Ha, do I hear optimism? That sounds like a good argument for carrying on.'

'That ain't the way I meant it, Grover. Seems that's the way broke-down bozos who call themselves prospectors like to tell it, claiming it was their bad luck to have stopped fifteen feet short. Like fishermen and their one that got away.'

The two of them walked away from the mine, down a slope to a thicket. Deep within the foliage Lang knelt and swept soil from a square of wood. He raised it to reveal a collection of similar bags. He added the new one, replaced the cover and scooped soil over it.

'And how much does that add up to in total?' Crawford asked as they walked back up the grade.

'We should get around five hundred for the lot. Not a fortune but it'll keep us going.'

There was a bite in the air the next morning when Lang awoke. Crawford had been right about the weather. And it was changing for the worse. Winter was coming early this year. He emerged from his tent to find the ground cold, icy and hostile. He rubbed his hands and stamped his feet before heading to their open-air kitchen. They had had the foresight to keep the kindling under cover so it didn't take long to get the fire going. Crawford liked his sleep so it was Lang's habit to make early morning preparations. He placed the coffee pot over the flames and went to check the horses in the home-made lean-to. Only to note that there was a horse missing.

He dashed to Crawford's tent and pulled open the flap. It was empty.

He scanned the valley. No sign of him anywhere. His companion was not the type to pursue chores without request or instruction. So he wasn't woodcutting. Then he saw the tracks. There had been light fall of snow during the night. Enough for a rider and horse laden with gold to leave their marks.

He slithered down to their cache in thicket. Snow had been scooped away and only two sad-looking bags remained.

He went back to Crawford's tent and cast an eye over its dishevelled contents. Not even a goodbye note.

Minutes later he was hunched over the fire, his hands clasped round a hot mug. Hell, he should have seen it coming. He knew what Crawford was like. He'd been a shady hornswoggler at Alton, a sharp dealer, feeling no remorse in living off the backs of his fellow prisoners. And, although Lang didn't know details, there'd been strong hints that the guy had only donned the grey to escape some suspicious entanglement he'd brought upon himself.

But it had never occurred to Lang that the young man would pull his stunts on his old pal. You live and learn, he told himself.

Come lunch-time he had made up his mind. Crawford had been right. There had to be diggings more profitable than here. He saddled his horse, loaded up the pack-animals and with one last look at what had been their home for three months he headed down the grade.

6

The cemetery stood on a hill beside the town where a man was standing beside a grave. Grover Lang contemplated the words crudely scratched on the wooden marker.

'Sorry I couldn't make it in time, Jim, but you know I did my best.'

At forty his brother had still had some good years to live. Lang had been engrossed in work when a message had come through that his younger brother was gravely ill. He had set off as soon as he could but it was a long stretch from the depths of Arizona to the small Mexican border town and by the time he had made it his brother had gone.

Six months had passed since Crawford had vamoosed and Lang had been left to pursue his explorations alone. But it had been worth it. He'd hit a lode in Arizona. So good, in fact, that it was proving too much for one man. That was when he got the word his brother was seriously ill. And he had dropped everything to make the journey.

Lang studied the marker a little longer, patted it meditatively, then walked slowly down the hill.

At the bottom a voice broke into his thoughts.

'Señor Lang.'

It was an old Mexican with sombrero in his hands standing near a derelict wagon. 'My name is Ignacio, *señor*. It was I who notified you.'

'Thanks. How did you know of me?'

'Your brother, he spoke of you much, *señor*.'

'And how did you know how to contact me?'

'He had a letter with your details.'

Lang nodded. 'For you to send me the note, that must have meant the two of you were close.'

'*Sí, señor*.'

Lang pushed some bills into the Mexican's hand. 'It was good of you to let me know.' He looked back up the hill. 'I guess you did your best for him.'

'It was my duty, *señor*. Señor Lang, he was a good man.'

'You were with him when he died?'

'*Sí, señor*.'

The American looked back at the town, noticed a cantina. 'I know nothing of the circumstances of his death. Will you do me one last service, Ignacio? Accompany me to yonder cantina where we can drink to his memory and you can maybe tell me the details.'

The man looked apprehensive, threw furtive

glances this way and that. 'In such a place one never knows who might be listening, *señor*. It is better that we talk out here. *Sigame por favor.*'

Lang watched the old man shuffle behind the wagon and squat, his back against a wheel.

'You know anything about your brother's time here?' the man asked when Lang was hunkered in similar fashion beside him.

'No. Just that he came down here over the border to avoid the war. We argued over that because at first I thought he was acting like a coward. But I should have known better. He said it was a matter of principle; that he couldn't fight to defend slavery. We argued over that, too. I said it was a fight about the right to secede, not slavery. But he didn't see it that way and hit the trail. I didn't know where he went until I got a message that he was down here. Since then we've exchanged a few letters.'

'I remember such letters, *señor*. When one came he would read it slowly over and over.'

'Last I heard he married a Mexican girl and that there was to be a child. That reminds me, where are they?'

'Juanita. We shall talk of her later.'

'When?'

'After we have talked of the manner of his dying.'

'I'm listening.'

'You know our country is in the middle of a rebellion, *señor*?'

'I've heard a little, but I thought the fighting was centred around Mexico City, much further south from here.'

'That is where the main action is, *señor*, but resistance is developing all around the country.'

'Against the French?'

'And others. The French tried for years to take over Mexico. Our beloved General Seguin defeated them back in '62 but our victory only delayed their invasion and last year they successfully occupied our country. *Asi*, they installed Maximilian on the throne, declaring the foreigner as Emperor of All Mexico. Huh, he and his wife Carlota are just puppets of the hated Napoleon of France. Anyway, President Juárez is in hiding, keeping the legitimate government functioning in the name of the Republic and organizing rebellion.'

'How did my brother fit into all this?'

'There was a rebel group based in our town. Maximilian's men heard of it; they have their spies everywhere. They came – I don't whether they were French, Austrians or Belgians – and there was much shooting. But the foreigners have superior weapons and there was much killing. When the fighting was over they took all the remaining young men from the village, lined them up against the wall and shot them.'

'My brother included?'

'I am afraid so.'

'So that's the way he went,' Lang said contemplatively.

The old man looked up the hill. 'The *señor* may have seen many new graves up there.'

'So my brother was one of the rebels.'

'No, *señor*. He was sympathetic to their cause but he was not active. Played no part in our politics. He protested to the soldiers that he was an American citizen but it made no difference.'

'But your letter to me said that he was ill, gravely ill.'

'*Sí*, he survived the shooting and that is when I sent the letter. He was ill from his wounds. But he died shortly afterwards. I sent another letter to tell you so.'

'I left as soon as I got the first letter.' The American dropped his head. 'The second is probably waiting for me back home in Arizona.' He looked up at the sky. 'Did he suffer much?'

'He fell into a long sleep from which he never recovered.'

'And what about Juanita and the baby? I must see them.'

'Of course, *señor*, I will take you to them.'

She was a pretty woman and Lang could see how his brother had been attracted to her. The infant had her swarthy skin but the blue eyes were Jim's. With her husband gone the woman could no longer pay rent so she and the child were now living with Ignacio and his wife. The old man didn't have to say but Lang could tell by the impoverished conditions that two extra mouths to feed imposed a burden on the old couple. Not made easier by the political upheavals through which the people were now living.

After living with Jim the woman had a fair grasp of English and Lang spoke with her for a long time about her life with his brother.

By the time he had finished off a meal supplied by Ignacio's wife, Lang had made up his mind. 'Listen, Juanita, I want to take you away from all this and look after you and the boy. I have a place in Arizona and I'm doing well. I think you'd like it there.'

The girl looked askance. 'That is a long way from home, *señor*. I have never travelled far before.'

'I know, but it'll give you a chance to start a new life. And with you being family I feel a duty to do right by the two of you.' He also felt a duty to ensure that his nephew was raised in conditions better than the squalor in which they now lived, but he left that sentiment unsaid.

She looked at the old man. 'What do you think, Ignacio?' she said in Spanish.

'Señor Lang is a good man, like Jim. I think it would be for the best.'

She hesitated, then Lang smiled and prompted

her with, 'That is, if you don't mind little Jim being raised as a gringo.'

She smiled for the first time. 'I don't mind, *señor.*'

'Right, that's settled,' Lang said. 'We're gonna need a wagon for your possessions. Get your things together while I look for one.'

Scouting the town he eventually found what he needed, together with a couple of mules. They left the following morning.

The journey down had familiarized him with the geography so he had little problem working his way back to the frontier. The last town was as he remembered, a sprawl of adobes claimed from the desert.

'I'm gonna stock up on supplies and some tools,' he said, drawing in at the entrance to the town. Buying the wagon and mules had reminded him how much cheaper things were this side of the border. 'I'll try not to be long.'

Down an alley he found a store selling what he wanted. He returned to the wagon.

'Let us get quickly from here, *señor,*' Juanita said when he reappeared. 'It is a bad place.'

'Bad? How?'

'Bad things happen.'

'OK, I'll just load up. The store's not far.'

He steered the wagon along the drag and down the alley.

Some time later he had loaded his purchases and was settling back into the driving seat when he heard screams coming from somewhere along the main street. The screams were followed by gunfire, then more screams.

'Stay here,' he said, 'while I find out what's happening.'

He dropped to the ground and moved to the end of the alley. Cautiously he peered around the corner. There were crowds in the distance. Against a background of intermittent gunfire, soldiers were dragging men while womenfolk screamed. When he saw the men being herded against a wall, he'd seen enough. He'd already heard from Ignacio how things were conducted down here. He loped back down the alley.

'Take off the brake,' he said, grabbing the halters of the mules. He pushed at the animals, which reluctantly moved backwards. It was an awkward manoeuvre but eventually he got the vehicle clear of the alley. He returned to his seat and headed the wagon along the backs of the houses in parallel with the main drag.

Clear of the town he urged the mules to a trot over the rough red ground.

Some miles on there was a hefty clunk in the back. He checked the surrounding area to see they were under no immediate threat and pulled the ribbons to halt the mules. 'Sounds like something's loose back there. I'll see if the load needs restacking. Wouldn't like any of the bags to get ripped.'

He stared ahead. The river crossing would not be far away.

Then, by the side of the wagon, he threw open the tarp.

'What the—?'

Three Mexican faces looked up, fear writ in their eyes.

'*Per favor, señor,*' one said. Then added in faltering English, 'Do not give us away, *señor.*

Lang looked at Juanita. 'You know about this?'

'*Sí.* They climbed aboard when the wagon was in the alley and you went to investigate the shooting. They were fleeing for their lives.'

'You understand English?' Lang asked of his uninvited passengers.

'*Poco, señor.*'

'What's your name?'

'Miguel, *señor.* My *compadres,* they are Felipe and Rodrigo.'

Lang glanced around. 'Well, Miguel, there are no soldiers within sight. You can get out quite safely.'

The one named Miguel who seemed to be their spokesman peered cautiously over the tailboard. 'Soldiers still may come and we are in the open without cover. And there may be soldiers yet ahead. We would be grateful if we could stay aboard a little longer.'

Lang's face was stern. He had no objective other than to get out of this damn country as soon as possible and he didn't want extra encumbrances or to take any action that might bring risk to the boy and woman.

'Oh, please allow them to stay, Grover,' Juanita said. 'There's been enough killing and these are not evil men. They are humble Mexicans who just want the foreigners to leave our country.'

Lang sighed as he reflected. If only there had been someone like him around when his brother needed sanctuary.

'OK,' he said, 'I'll see what I can do. But keep quiet, don't move and keep your heads down. Remember, if we run into trouble you could jeopardize the life of the woman and child if you act rashly.'

'Anything you say, *señor.*'

When they got to the ferry the shooting had finished but the distant sounds of some commotion could still be heard.

'What is going on, *señor*?' the ferryman asked, his eyes probing their back trail.

'Don't ask me,' Lang said. 'I'm just a Yank trader passing through and ignorant of Mexican affairs.' The remote sound of a rifle being fired suddenly reached them and he gestured his head in its direction. 'More important I'm a man anxious to get his sister-in-law and young nephew to a place where folk ain't so gun-happy.'

The Mexican helped him manoeuvre the wagon on to the ferry and Lang breathed a sigh of relief as it eventually rolled on to American soil. He threw a comforting smile at Juanita.

A mile on he halted near a low area of rock and made a pretence of adjusting the tarp. 'We're clear of the river now, boys, but we can still be seen from there. So reckon it'll be a wise thing to stay put a mite longer.'

They hadn't rolled much further when Juanita said, 'We are being followed by soldiers.'

Lang threw a glance back and made out about a dozen green uniforms fast approaching at a gallop.

'What is going to happen?' she said in a distressed tone.

'Stay cool,' he said. 'They got no rights here.'

A couple of minutes passed before the first of the riders drew level.

'Pull in, *m'sieur*,' their leader shouted above the creaking of wheelrims.

Lang ignored the order but was brought to a standstill by the man firing ahead of the mules.

'Now what is your business?' the officer asked. 'And what do you have in the wagon?'

Lang eyed the unfamiliar ornate uniform. 'This is American land. You have no jurisdiction here.'

'What is in the wagon?'

'Personal supplies,' Lang snapped. 'Not that it's

51

any of your affair. Far more important: what is your name and rank?'

For a moment the man was taken aback, then he said, 'Capitaine Boulanger at your service.' His voice was rigid with pride.

'Well, Capitaine Boulanger, you will not be aware of my standing in this community. I am a man of substance and influence. But what you do need to know is that I am a US national and you are illegally on US territory.'

The officer stiffened at the tone of authority in the American's voice.

But before he could get a reply past his lips, Lang went on: 'For some time the federal government has been concerned about foreign powers infringing Mexican sovereignty. Believe me, they are just waiting for an excuse to send an army across the Rio Grande to expel French intruders from an independent country within the American hemisphere. If you interfere with me in any way – namely, by preventing a US citizen going about his rightful business on US soil – you will give them that reason. Do you want to be held responsible for creating an international incident?'

The captain grunted disdainfully. 'You are speaking to ten rifles, *monsieur*.'

'I can count. But the number of your weaponry is immaterial. And so is the fact that we are seemingly out of sight of any witnesses, because my presence here is known and so is yours. If anything should happen to me, it will not be long before whatever you perpetrate is discovered. Of course, by then you may be well gone but your action will have been enough to trigger an armed response across the river by my government against yours – and you will be known to your superiors to be the cause. You may have heard of the old saying: do not poke a sleeping tiger with a stick.'

He made a display of surveying the soldiers before looking back at the officer. 'So think twice before you give your next order, *mon capitaine.*'

The man harrumphed. He stared hard at Lang for a spell, then waved his arm ordering his troops back.

Lang flicked the traces for his mules to proceed and didn't look back lest the soldiers saw him, a movement that would likely make him look apprehensive.

'What is your standing in the community?' Juanita whispered.

'None that I know of,' Lang answered, 'but that ain't the point.'

A little later a muffled voice came from under the tarp. 'Have they gone, *señor?*'

'Just keep your heads down and stay quiet a little longer.'

7

Eventually the wagon fetched up on the outskirts of a small town.

'OK, you can come out,' Lang said. 'There are no soldiers about.'

One by one, the three dropped down to the sandy soil.

'We are forever in your debt, *señor*,' Miguel said.

'Forget it. I'm pleased to oblige.' Lang looked back. 'It was bastards in that uniform – or ones like it – killed my brother for no reason.'

'Your brother, he was with rebels?'

'No. He just got in the way.'

'If we had *mucho* dollar, they would be yours, *señor*. But as it is, we just about got clear with our lives and little else. So all we can do is give you our thanks.'

'Your thanks are enough.' He eyed them and asked, 'What are you going to do now?'

'We cannot go back yet so we will stay on this side of the border for the time being. Maybe we can earn some dinero at the same time. It would be good if we could take something back to help with the cause. Earning some money and keeping away from Maximilian's men would – how you say? – kill two birds with one stone.'

'Can't help you on that score. I'm a stranger in these parts myself and we got ways to go. Well, the best of luck, fellers – and *adios*.'

The men waved their goodbyes and headed to the town.

'What now, *señor*?' Juanita asked.

Lang peered ahead. 'As I recall this is the last town for quite a spell. Figure we should find lodgings for the night and head out in the morning.'

They found adequate premises with facilities for them to wash up. The proprietor, an burly Irishman, was welcoming and prepared a filling meal.

'You travelled far?' he asked as he cleared the table.

'Came up from Mexico,' Lang said. 'Had some family business down there.'

'You were wise to get the hell out of there. From what I hear it is not a safe place to be at the moment. Bullets flying in all directions. Some rebels are trying to overthrow the government.'

'Yeah. Saw evidence of it.'

'Wouldn't be so bad if they kept themselves to themselves but it's spilling over the border.'

'What do you mean?'

'Whenever you get trouble on that scale, ordinary folks are gonna try to get away from it. We get loads of 'em, you know, just plain folk with their families coming up here looking for safety.'

'Here, in this town?'

'Yeah. Some stay, others move on. If that ain't bad enough we get trigger-happy *rurales* scouring the Mex quarter looking for rebels.

'*Rurales?* What are they? Soldiers?'

'Kind of. The Mexican Rural Guard is what they call themselves. Claim they've got a right to cross the border to see if we're harbouring known revolutionaries. Say they're just Mexicans sorting out Mexican business and don't aim to cause trouble for any Americans.'

'They still got no right.'

'You try telling them that.'

'What do our authorities have to say about it? It's tantamount to invasion of US territory.'

The Irishman grunted sardonically. 'What authorities? Ain't no authorities out here. Huh, we ain't even got our own peace officer.'

As Lang lay in bed trying to sleep, his mind trawled through the events of the day. By the time sleep had taken over, an idea had formed. The result was he was up at the crack of dawn, intent on exploring a possibility. After a quick breakfast he made his way to the burgeoning Mexican quarter and enquired after the three strangers from the previous day.

People were uneasy at first but the conversations were overheard and the one he recognized as Miguel appeared in a doorway.

'This man is OK. He is a friend of ours.' He gestured for Lang to follow him back into the interior.

The faces of Rodrigo and Felipe lit up when they recognized their visitor.

'The purpose of my visit is to inform you that you are not safe here,' Lang said. '*Rurales* are making lightning raids looking for men such as yourselves. They're not supposed to operate on this side of the border but seems nothing can be done about that.'

'Thank you for warning us but we have been told of that, *señor*. It is our intention to travel further north this very day.'

Lang cast his eyes over the three men, then said, 'I've had an idea. Maybe we could be of mutual benefit to each other.'

'What is the idea, *señor*?' Miguel asked.

'I am in need of young, muscular arms. Like those of you and your *compadres*. You are in need of a place that will keep the Mexican soldiers out of your hair for a spell. I can provide you with such a place where none of these invaders can find you for as along as you like. At the same time you can earn money. I cannot say how much – certainly enough to get by, maybe more. But don't be feared. It's hard but honest toil.'

Miguel looked at his friends and noted agreement in their faces. 'That is more than we would wish for, *señor*. Where is this place?'

Lang chuckled. 'It is a secret place and if I describe its location it will be a secret no longer. But, rest assured, I will tell you when the time is ripe. I cannot say more at present. If you want to join me, we're gonna have to trust each other. *Comprende?*'

'You have already had our lives in the palm of your hand, *señor*. One cannot trust a man more than that. We will never forget what you have done – and you will find us equally honourable in our dealings with you.'

Lang nodded. 'That I believe.'

8

Grover Lang dropped to the ground just before the train stopped so that he was the first passenger to alight. It was a deliberate ploy and so much part of his routine on his frequent round trips to Dana City, ten miles up the track, that he gave the action no thought. He crossed to the station building and settled into a seat under an awning as the train came to a halt. To all appearances he was engrossed in fumbling with a pipe and match but in reality he was using the activity as a strategy so that he could scrutinize his fellow passengers as they disembarked. He casually puffed on the pipe until he was alone, all travellers having departed either on the short walk to town or spirited away by waiting transport.

None of them had seemed to be concerned with him; but just in case one of them was maintaining a similar pretence he had made a mental note of

59

every face for possible future reference.

He walked through the small settlement of Apache Flats till he reached his apartment on the edge of town. Set back only a few yards from the main drag it occupied the ground floor of a small block. In choosing it on his first arrival in town over three years ago he had had only his own needs to meet. It had been adequate for those and he hadn't minded its physical restrictions as he spent a large portion of his time away. Nor had he minded the confined space at the back, just big enough to accommodate his horse, mule and buggy.

Juanita naturally, having only ever known severely cramped conditions, had been quite happy with it from the very moment she had crossed the threshold some two years since. But Lang hankered for something bigger, more fitting as he saw it, for the accommodation of three people, one a fast-growing boy. For this reason he had recently taken out a mortgage to buy a two-storey house. Its location was ideal. Three miles out of town in the direction of Dana City, it was far enough away for one not to feel hemmed in, yet near enough to Apache Flats for the purchase of necessities and some social life if circumstances arose. The interior was spacious and it was set in a large tract of land, which he foresaw providing an admirable adventure playground for an energetic, imaginative young lad. The place had been empty for some time and it was on his agenda to render it suitable for the housing of what he now saw as his family.

Juanita greeted him as he came through the narrow doorway of the apartment and they exchanged brother and sister kisses to the cheek. Little Jim was now a capable walker and came toddling forward. Lang went into a crouch with his arms open and, emitting a lengthy 'Wheee!', scooped up his little nephew. He carried him to the centre of the room and sat him on the floor.

'What's Uncle Grover got?' he said, taking a carved wooden horse from his pocket and giving it to the child to explore.

'How have things been?' he asked, patting the boy's head and rising to his feet.

'Fine. You transacted your business OK?' she replied, the enunciation of words showing a vast improvement in her pronunciation of English.

'As usual went like clockwork.' He nodded to the kitchen. 'Something smells good in there. I'm starving.'

'You'll have to be patient. It's not quite ready.'

After he had exchanged his sober business clothing for range gear he went out back and checked the animals.

That evening they were seated before a log fire, he relaxing with a drink and pipe while Juanita attended to her sewing.

'I was thinking,' he said. 'Maybe tomorrow we

could go out for a picnic.'

'Don't you have to get back to work?'

'It can wait another day. We can ride out to Moonbeam and kill two birds at a time.'

He had dubbed his purchase Moonbeam on a spur of whimsy. He had feared in past low moments that his lonely prospecting was nothing more than chasing moonbeams, so he saw it as a fitting name for the house, bought as it was from the very proceeds of 'chasing moonbeams'.

'I can use the occasion to do some measuring while we're out there,' he continued. 'I'd also like to give it a final once-over before I start to formulate a programme of redecoration. And you can give me the benefit of your advice on what needs doing and what you would like to see done.'

'I can offer advice with pleasure but I would I would not presume to tell you what I would like. It is your house after all, *señor.*'

'How many times do I have to tell you? You're my sister-in-law. So less of the *señor*. It's Grover.'

'I look forward to it, *Señor Grover.*'

He harrumphed noisily and began to investigate the contents of his pipe with feigned intensity. 'Right, that's settled.'

They confined their time out at the house to the morning as he had reserved the afternoon for preparation of his next lengthy work period. He changed into his range gear and toured the town buying coffee and other supplies.

'Not in the way, are they?' he asked on his return after he'd stacked his purchases in the kitchen. 'I'm afraid there's not much room as it is.'

'Of course not,' Juanita said with a smile. 'It's only until tomorrow.'

'Damn.' he said as he surveyed the bags. 'Forgot flour. Miguel and the boys will never forgive me. Good job I have to go back to the stores anyway.'

Once again in the main street he bought several bags of flour and three boxes of cigars. Last of all he made for the gunsmith's.

'What you got in the shape of a long-range hunting gun, Jed?' he asked.

'The Wesson, Mr Lang,' the man said, pointing to a long-barrelled rifle on the rack. 'Best in the store. Good for half a mile, they say.'

'Fine piece of weaponry. Can I test it?'

'My range out back ain't big enough to give it a proper test, Mr Lang, but you're more than welcome to take it to a more fitting spot.'

Minutes later Lang was on the outskirts of town. He lined up on a distant cactus and put a couple of shots through it.

'I'll take it,' he said, back in the store.

'I'm sorry I ain't got a proper holster for it.'

'No matter. As long as it's wrapped in something substantial and protective. It's got a piece of some

63

travelling to do.'

He was struggling along the boardwalk, encumbered by his unanticipated burden of extra bags, when he heard a voice.

'Let me help you with them.'

He turned round to identify the speaker.

'Monte!'

'Howdy, Grover. Long time, no see.'

9

'Jeez, you made me jump, Monte,' Lang said, straining to speak under the weight of his packages.

'Sorry, pal,' Crawford said.

'Didn't see you. So unexpected.'

'Here, let me help you with your trappings,' Crawford said, looking around as if to check they weren't being seen. He relieved Lang of a couple of heavy bags. 'Which way, Captain?'

'Must say, this is one hell of a surprise,' Lang said when they were inside the apartment.

'Surprise for me too, pal.' The visitor's voice lowered in contrition. 'Figure I was the last person you would want to see, me having scooted and all.'

At that Juanita came in from the kitchen wiping her hands on a cloth.

'This is my friend Monte Crawford,' Lang said by way of introduction. 'Haven't seen him in a coon's age.'

'I thought I heard voices.'

'This is Juanita.'

'Howdy, ma'am.'

'How's little Jim,' Lang asked as he placed one of the packages on the table.

'Afternoon nap. This morning's outing has exhausted the poor little *señorito*.'

Crawford looked quizzical. 'Your boy? Hey, I didn't figure you'd have a family and all. Never thought you'd have been able to fit plain, simple domesticity in between all those big ideas of yours.'

'Don't run ahead of yourself,' Lang chided. 'Juanita's my brother's widow. Little Jimmy, he's my nephew. I'm sure I mentioned I had a brother, Jim.'

'Oh, yeah.'

As Crawford showed no interest in the circumstances of his brother's passing, Lang let the topic pass, then asked, 'So, Monte, how long you been in town?'

'Rode in but half an hour ago.'

'In that case, reckon you could sink a coffee, right?'

'I'll see to it,' Juanita said. 'You *hombres* make yourself comfortable in the other room. You must have *mucho* to talk about.'

Lang ushered his friend to a chair.

'Mighty cosy,' Crawford said, leaning back in the seat and taking in the room.

'It is.'

66

Crawford threw a glance at the entrance to the kitchen and said in a lowered voice, 'Look, Grover. Real sorry about leaving you in the lurch and making off with the gold. Been on my mind to pay you back ever since. I was only borrowing it, you understand.'

Lang nodded. 'I see. So that's why you've gone to the trouble of finding me out?'

'No. Hell, wish I could pay the loan back right now – you know me, it's been on my conscience all these years? How long's it been now?'

'I'd say around four years.'

'Yeah, four years. Long time, but fact is I'm kinda short at the moment.'

'Don't worry about it. Like you never failed to remind me out in Montana, it wasn't much. True, we weren't making our fortunes out of the operation. Anyways, that's water under the bridge.'

At that point Juanita brought in the coffee and cookies. 'Don't worry about me, gentlemen. I'll get out of your way. You'll still have lots to talk about and I've got things to do.'

Crawford grabbed some cookies before the plate had hit the table, and proceeded to wolf them down.

'One thing I can say about Juanita,' Lang said. 'She sure makes a good biscuit.'

When she had left the room Lang eyed his visitor. 'So, how did you find me?'

'Pure luck, pal. I wasn't looking for you at this time. Got other things on my mind. No, happens by chance I'd just rode into town and suddenly saw my old buddy. Hell, I couldn't believe my eyes. Should go and see him, I thought. Chance to mend broken bridges and all.'

As they finished off the refreshments they brought each other up to date on their lives, at least what they saw fit to share.

'So, what brings you out to Arizona?' Lang asked when they had exchanged summaries. 'I know you hankered for the sun. But why Apache Flats of all places?'

'Just drifting. Anyways, I could ask you the same thing. Why Apache Flats?'

'It's as good as any.'

Crawford looked around the room. 'Must say, my old pal seems to be doing all right for himself.'

'I think you're being polite. OK, it's better than the tents in which we lodged but this place is no great shakes. Nevertheless, I make out.'

'The place yours?'

'Leased.' He emptied his cup. 'You'll be staying for a meal, won't you? Juanita is the best of cooks, as you have already experienced.'

'That's real kind.'

'The least I can do for an old *compadre*.'

'You mean that – "old *compadre*" – after the stunt I pulled on you?'

68

Lang grunted. 'Sure. You're a young rascal right enough, Monte, no gainsaying that. But they say a fellow has to take the rough with the smooth as far as his pals are concerned.'

'I need to get more supplies from town while the stores are still open,' Lang said when they'd eaten. There was always some small item he'd forgotten when getting ready for an extended trip. 'You come with me?'

Crawford was standing by the window, his head angled near the curtains.

'The evening is young,' Lang went on. 'We can have an hour or two relaxing in the saloon afterwards. Four years. We still got a lot of talking to do.'

Crawford's brow puckered as he returned from the window. 'Any talking we do, I'd prefer we do it here.'

Lang smiled. 'Monte, it hasn't eluded me that you've been antsy ever since you showed up.'

'Antsy? What do you mean.'

'I know you well enough. Enough to tell when you're extra edgy. Your ears cock every time there's a sound from outside. And like just then – that's not the first time you've checked the window.'

Crawford smiled. 'Hell, Grover, can't hide anything from you, can I?' He sighed resignedly. 'Reckon I'd better come clean. Truth of the matter,

I got folks after me.'

Lang shook his head. 'Will you ever change? What you been up to now? Conned some gullible priest out of his charity cents?'

'More serious than that. Payroll job out in New Mexico.'

Lang stiffened. 'Payroll? You mean – real thieving?'

'Yeah. 'Fraid so.'

'I know you as a sharp but didn't figure you were the kind to go so far. Attempting to take a payroll, that's another league.'

'I know, but I was desperate, Grover.'

'Still the same old Monte.'

The visitor dropped into a chair and stared at flames dancing in the fireplace. 'Anyways, it all went wrong. Unfortunately there was some shooting. I managed to get away but I figure the law are on my tail.'

'Figure? You're not sure?'

'They'll be after me all right but I reckon I'm well ahead of them as I ain't seen nobody on my back trail. But can't be too careful. Which is why I'm trying to lose myself out here.'

'Have you considered giving yourself up? Coming clean will be taken into consideration and it might not end up as bad you think.'

'Ain't in my nature to trust anybody in the law business. Men with badges or judges.'

'This payroll job, how serious was it?'

'One of the guards was shot. Don't know if he made it. But if he died that makes it a federal case so state and territorial lines won't stop them. That's why Arizona, even a nowhere place like Apache Flats, might not be safe for me.'

'This is serious. The one who was shot – you did it?'

No, it was my pal. Fact, *he* started the gunplay. Myself, don't cotton to using shooters on a job. It puts up the ante from the law's point of view.'

'And where is your pal?'

'Huh, they put a bullet into him. Looked like a goner last time I seed him.' He shook his head. 'Trouble follows me around.'

'Monte, trouble doesn't follow you around – you go looking for it.'

'Yeah. So, cutting to the chase, I'm looking for a place to hole up. Since I've come across you – and now we've patched things up between us – I been wondering if you'd see your way clear to me lying low here.'

'Don't like the notion of that all,' Lang said and went to the window. 'As you've already pointed out, Apache Flats is a small town. If federal marshals do come riding in and decide to comb the whole place, it won't be long before they're turning my apartment over.'

'I told you, ain't seen anyone on my back trail.'

71

'As far as the law's concerned you never can tell, especially in the light of the scale of the transgression you've described. The long arm stretches far and wide these days, with the telegraph and all.'

He gestured around the room. 'And what have I got to offer you in terms of a hideaway? A cramped apartment and a poky lean-to out back. Look how confined it is. Should lawmen, especially federals, nose around, they'll soon root you out of a cupboard or from under the bed. On top of that they'd know there was no way you could be hiding here without my knowing so I'd be taken as an accessory. I've got to think of Juanita and Jimmy should I get into trouble. But you probably hadn't thought of that.'

'Grover, you're my last chance. I can't run for ever.'

Lang went to the window and watched the last of the shoppers heading for home. After some consideration he sighed and said, 'Where's your horse?'

'Hitched to a rail in town.'

'Well, that needs to be out of the way as soon as possible. Tell you what I'll do. I'll return to the stores and buy some small item which will give me the opportunity to see if there are any law officers around. If it's clear I'll collect the horse and put it in my lean-to for the time being. At least, the animals' quarters can't be seen easily from town. And it'll give me time to think.'

The younger man slapped his friend's shoulders. 'Grover, you're real white.'

'Yeah,' Lang said, and crossed to the door.

'I knew I could rely on you, pal.'

Lang paused at the door. 'And while I'm away, no point in searching my place, *pal.* Juanita won't like it and there's nothing worth the taking.'

'Listen,' he said when he was back in the house after completing his task on the drag. 'I've been putting some thought into it. I'm going away tomorrow. You can come with me. It'll get you out of the apartment. I don't want Juanita and the kid involved in any of this. You can change your appearance in some way to get clear of town. I've got spare clothes you can choose from.'

'A change of clothes won't fool anybody for long.'

'We'll be setting out before daybreak so there's little chance of your being seen anyway. We should be able to manage that. And once we've got you out of town things should run OK. Then you can hole up as long as you like.'

'Where we going?'

'It's too complicated to explain, but where we're headed nobody will never find you.'

10

There were no rays reflecting off the underside of clouds to rouse the local roosters as Crawford pulled out from the alley alongside the Lang apartment. In a change of clothing and with his hat pulled low over his eyes, he rode out alone to a spot carefully described by Lang.

Even in the blackness the position was easily identified by the pungent odour of greasewood. By the time he reached it there was enough light from the false dawn for him to see the clump of evil-smelling vegetation, the source of the smell, that he had been told to look out for.

He turned off the trail as instructed by Lang and eventually came to his second landmark. It was an out-of-the-way place, far from the trail and even in daylight unseen from town. With his horse tethered to a cottonwood he hunkered down and leant against the trunk.

While he waited he lit a cigarette. Despite his perplexity about the nature of the exercise and the fact he had put himself completely in the hands of his friend, there was a degree of relaxation in his demeanour. On the one hand he was sure he hadn't been seen leaving town and, on the other, he had complete trust in his old buddy.

His puzzlement increased when he noted Lang approaching – with two heavily laden burros in tow.

They joined up and rode further away from town with Lang repeatedly looking about, especially to their rear. For a long time they kept to the plain, riding parallel with the rocky terrain to the west. After an hour Lang reined in and dropped down. He took out some fieldglasses and very carefully studied the horizon at all compass points.

'I've been keeping a weatherleye,' Crawford said. 'I don't think anybody's seen us.'

'I have to be sure we're not being followed,' Lang said.

'Thanks for being careful, pal.'

'It's for my reasons as well as yours.'

Satisfied they still had that part of the universe to themselves, Lang took out large leather shoes from his saddle-bag.

'Reduces sign,' he said as he set about fixing them to all of the animals' hoofs in turn. When the task was complete he mounted and turned his horse sharply to one side. The sharpness of the angle meant that he was working to some well-established plan but Crawford reckoned there would not be much point in asking questions.

Eventually Crawford drew level with Lang and the latter pointed to the shale over which he had decided to travel. 'It is important that we leave no track,' he said.

For a while they back-tracked at an obtuse angle, getting nearer to the rocky outcrops, which were cracked by massive fissures.

Coming to one of the canyon entrances Lang dismounted and repeated his procedure with the fieldglasses.

'OK,' he said, hauling himself back into the saddle. He nudged his horse into the gorge. From there they progressed between the castles of stone until they emerged into an open area with Lang still regularly scrutinizing their surroundings. Part way across the flat Lang turned and headed towards uplands. At the end of the long, slow rise he chose yet another large gully.

'This is Deadman's Pass,' he said. 'Rightly named. It leads to a network of deceptive canyons out of which not many men have returned.'

Passing through the opening, they faced a steep downward grade of some 400 feet. Not only was the steepness a challenge but descent was over stones and shale. They dismounted and made their way slowly downward. Reaching the level floor they mounted again and proceeded amid clusters of piñon trees.

At first Crawford couldn't understand what was so mysterious about the route. So far it had been arduous but straightforward. Even when they entered an area serving as the confluence for incoming gullies, they merely proceeded along the main canyon.

But from time to time they would enter an area of several intersecting canyons and Lang would select one which, to a stranger, had nothing to distinguish it from all the others. And so, after a handful of such turnings, Crawford began to realize the danger of the intricacies of Deadman's Pass and the significance of its name. Any exhausted visitor without water could easily get lost and would quickly find his last resting place.

Come evening they turned into a canyon which took them to a valley where they set up camp. Lang's familiarity with the area was obvious as he had ridden straight to a perfect site sheltered by oak trees and complete with running water in the shape of a shallow stream.

'You got a map of this route?' Crawford asked, when they had finished their meal.

Lang smiled and touched his forehead. 'That's my only map.'

'I don't know how you do it. After the first ten miles it was all looking the same to me.'

'There lies the difference. Every man to his trade. I told you I was trained as a geologist.' He waved his arm at the rugged walls that loomed over them. 'Just like a horse wrangler will tell you no two horses are alike, each of these formations has its own distinctive personality to someone like me.'

'As long as a man's got a map, he doesn't have to be a specialist.'

'I've told you there are no maps. At least not that I know of. No one has seen fit to chart it. In our day of travelling, have you seen anything worth coming out here for? A man needs a reason, a strong reason, before he ventures into a hostile region such as this.'

'Then what's the attraction to you?'

Lang smiled. 'Are you not satisfied that I am providing you with the perfect hidey-hole?'

'Well, sure. And I'm grateful. That's why I've refrained from asking questions, but I tell you, Grover: every step we take further into this labyrinth my curiosity ratchets up another notch.'

'You know my dreams. Well, they finally came true; I found myself a lode.'

In the firelight he saw Crawford's eyes widen a little.

'I call it the Santa Maria,' Lang went on. 'So you won't just be hiding away, wasting your time.'

'Like Montana?'

'Listen, do you want to hide away or not?'

'OK.'

'No, it's not like Montana. You pull your weight and you'll come out of here with enough dollars to tide you over. With a bit of luck, there'll be enough to distract you from your lawless escapades. The boys and I could do with another pair of hands. Monte, this *is* the big one. The richest source of gold I ever did see.'

Crawford's eyes were now really wide. 'A big one, huh? You'd cut me in? After the way I've treated you?'

'At bottom we're pals. OK, you've twisted me but you were at rock bottom. I understand that. Anyways, what you took was peanuts.'

'Now I understand the hefty amount of effort you put into making sure we weren't being followed. It wasn't just for my sake.'

The young man lit a cigarette. 'Do you store the stuff at the mine?'

'No, I get it assayed and sold regularly. That's what I was doing when you came across me at Apache Flats: returning from a delivery.'

Crawford thought about it. 'Then there's an assayer in Apache Flats who has you as a regular customer; and knows there's a lode in the locality. Do you trust him? Even if he's trustworthy – it's a small town – he only has to let something slip and news would spread like wildfire.'

'No worries on that score. Nobody knows. I take

79

the train out to Dana City and do my dealing there. It's a big place and they don't know me from Adam. I use the bank there so no suspicions are aroused back in Apache Flats. And I always ensure I'm not being followed from Dana.'

'And the mine's secure while you're away?'

Lang chuckled. 'Who's gonna stumble on it out here? I've been working it for three years with no problem. Nobody's going to find it. That's because I take care. Besides I have a group of very capable men there.'

'Others? You trust them?'

Lang yawned. 'No more questions. You'll get all your queries answered when we get there. And we need some rest in preparation for tomorrow's riding.'

'You mean there's a load more travelling to do through this hell?'

Lang lay down and closed his eyes. 'Hey, pal. That's another question.'

They set out at dawn. At times the canyon had a breadth of a hundred yards, at others it was no wider than to allow a couple of horses to pass.

Some walls slanted away, others went straight upgrasping at the sky with stony fingers, while at other places rock ominously overhung their passage.

Throughout the morning they twisted this way

and that, threading a way through the giant maze. Then, at one of the confluences of cross-cutting canyons, Lang turned towards a narrow crack with no visible passageway other than that for water to tumble through. They dismounted and made their way up through the pebble-bottomed stream. After half an hour of arduous ascent Crawford became aware of a distant rumble.

'Sounds like bad weather's on the way,' he said.

Several yards ahead, Lang ignored the comment and pressed on upwards.

But in time Crawford was aware that the sound was unbroken and louder.

'What's that?' he yelled, pausing to concentrate on the sound as it echoed between the stone walls.

'Don't worry,' Lang shouted back.

Eventually they emerged from the narrow crack to find themselves in a flat section, small but wide enough for them to step clear of the stream. The noise was now quite loud and the moisture in the air and dampness on the rock walls enabled Crawford to guess its source. When they followed the rivulet round a bend his guess was confirmed. They entered a large open plateau that held a pool fed by a narrow sparkling waterfall which seemed to reach to the sky itself. Most of the water from the pool was gushing out at the far end. The rivulet in which they had been soaking their boots for the last hour was a mere secondary runoff.

Crawford was puzzled. The only exits from the clearing were the two outflows. With the main outlet constituting a raging torrent, the only visible access to the area was the watery climb they had just made.

The noise was too great for him to ask any questions of his companion. But he didn't have to because Lang walked towards the waterfall, swinging his arm as an indication that he should be followed. And then he was gone.

Gingerly Crawford approached the cascade, bending his head as he neared in an attempt to see where his companion had disappeared. Between the falling water and the rock there was a natural corridor. Feeling hesitant, he paused at the entrance, keeping a firm grip on the bridle of his similarly nervous horse. Through the mist he could see Lang beckoning him on. By the time he had started to move the man had disappeared again.

Shielding his horse from the torrent by walking him against the wall, he slowly edged forward. Midway there was a fissure. He peered through it and could see Lang waiting for him. He led his horse into the narrow crack. The upward passage was of the same character as the one that had led to the waterfall – with the exception that it was relatively drier but noisier. Then another complication: a few yards in, the light disappeared so the journey had to be made in complete darkness.

Progress was very slow as he had to feel his way along the wall. Sweat broke out on Crawford's forehead, adding to the film of moisture already there. He had never liked enclosed spaces. The only thing that kept him going was the comforting clatter of Lang and horse some distance ahead. Even simple cupboards had been a no-go area for him in childhood games. Which was why he was especially thankful to see a spot of light before him.

When he reached the top he found Lang waiting.

'The main problem with that last stretch is the horses,' the older man said, noting the whiteness in the other's features. 'Being dark. But they did well.'

Out in the sun Crawford leant against the wall, reliving childhood nightmares.

'Nearly there,' Lang continued.

After a few moments Crawford followed him up a small grade between dense oak thickets.

'Look,' Lang said, pointing ahead as they came clear of the vegetation. Before them lay a sunken valley, maybe half a mile wide, its distant end not visible.

Crawford took in the towering crags that surrounded the place; it seemed to be completely sealed off from the world outside.

'This is it,' Lang said. 'We call it the Santa Maria.'

11

As he looked down into the valley, Crawford could
see little but sun-bleached earth and flowering
cactus at first. Then, squinting his eyes, he could
make out some movement at the base of a bluff in
the distance.

'That's it? Your camp?'

'Yes,'

'Don't you have a lookout?' he asked.

'Against what?' Lang said. He gestured with a
swing of his arm that they should descend. They
wended their way down between rocks until they
were at the base of the valley. As they neared the site
Crawford discerned laundry swinging lazily in the
slight breeze; then he saw a campfire and
ramshackle dwellings, some wooden contraptions
and a small but strange adobe construction.

'Hello the camp!' Lang shouted as they
approached.

'Ah, *señor*!' came the response, and there was much waving of hands and flashing of wide toothy smiles as three Mexicans began to home in from their different locations around the site.

Lang dismounted, made introductions, then took a bag from one of the burros. He opened it and took out a couple of pokes of coffee. Then, from the bottom of the bag, he extracted a package. He undid it and took out a large bundle of bills.

'Your wages,' he said, handing the cash to Miguel.

Crawford watched the Mexican count the money into two piles. The stuff was all in large denomination bills. There must have been a small fortune displayed on the sand.

'And how are things here?' Lang asked when the men had pocketed their earnings.

'No problems, *señor*,' Rodrigo said. 'Lady Nature still provides her bounty.'

Lang nodded in satisfaction. 'So we still haven't reached the end of the seam?'

'No, *señor*.

'There's flour, jerky, butter and other eats,' Lang said, pointing to the mule. 'Plus a treat: Juanita's baked a load of bread and your favourite Mex-style pastries.'

Felipe eagerly began to unpack the food. 'Ha – beans, cheese!' he exclaimed, kissing his fingers.

Lang threw a glance at Crawford. 'I sometimes

85

think they value the vittles more than the money. Come on, let's help Felipe – he's our unofficial quartermaster – get the provisions into the store.'

The store was a large niche in the rock not far from the campfire. When they had stacked the new additions Crawford looked them over closely.

'No drink?' he concluded.

'No. Don't allow any on the site. Booze makes men unpredictable and bad workers.'

'Not even a spot of tequila for the Mexes?'

'My Mexes don't need it. They are driven men. They work hard and they appreciate the money it brings them. And they value the opportunity to stay out of the limelight back home. That's all they need. They have a mission.'

As Crawford followed Lang down the slope his face bore a nonplussed expression as he contemplated a future without a drink.

'Right,' Lang said as they returned to the campfire where food was being prepared. 'Supper, then we find you a place to sleep.'

'Music to my ears. It's been a busy day.'

Next morning they rose early.

'Come on, Monte,' Lang said when they'd finished their breakfast. 'I'll give you a guided tour of the operation.'

He walked up the grade. 'Well, we have two operations going. Dry diggings deep in the bluff and this, an elaborate method of panning.'

He pointed to a long wooden contraption with water dribbling along to the end. 'I'll show you.'

When they got to it he pointed to the striplike slats that ran across the device. 'We call those riffle bars. The water coming out of the rock contains small particles of gold amongst the sludge and this thing, we call it a sluice box, is constructed to filter the lot out. The flow of water varies, depending on what the weather's been doing, but it works best when the water rushes down. All we have to do is extract the gold from the sludge that gathers in the bars.'

Crawford picked up a handful of silt. 'Can't see anything.'

'It's not exactly there for the picking.' Lang smiled. 'Takes a lot of sifting. But it's purer than the ore.'

He moved down the slope. 'Come. The other operation is deep in another cave.'

A hundred yards on he began clambering up the gradient and eventually entered an adit in the rock face from within which Crawford could detect the faint echo of tapping.

Lang took a lantern hanging just within the entrance and lit it. He led the way into the darkness. Deep inside they could see a glow in the distance; eventually they came across Rodrigo chipping at the rock face.

Lang pointed. 'See, there's a thin seam mixed in with the quartz. Not the biggest in history but it yields a steady supply.'

Back outside he pointed to a small adobe construction blackened around the top. 'The Mexicans built that. It's our smelter. We only run it for short periods because of the small amount of material we have to process. And then we usually do it during hours of darkness. It's not a good idea to have permanent smoke wafting up to attract attention. We never get folk passing by – but you never know.'

'Best not to tempt the devil, eh?' Crawford commented.

'It's our supplementary operation,' Lang went on. 'Of course, it's pure luck that the two sources are so close together. In a way they act as insurance. If either source dries up we can work the other for however long it lasts. So the site's got some kind of future.'

Crawford shook his head. 'That's what I call hitting the jackpot twice.'

'A jackpot suggests luck. While there's been luck in it, it took knowledge of geology to find them and then a heap of hard work to make them workable. What are you like with a hammer?'

'Dunno.'

Lang thumbed back to the adit. 'You'd be useful in there if you've a mind. But there's always something to do around camp. Besides ore extraction, there's cooking, maintaining and mending equipment, laundry, even vegetable growing. You can take your pick.'

Crawford grunted. 'Anything but working the land.'

'Why's that? It's honest toil. Gotta be done.'

'My folks were dirt farmers.'

'Didn't know that,' Lang said as he walked down the grade.

'Grubbing about with soil brings back too many bad memories. Ma was working the land when she died. I was very young then so I barely remember her. But I reckon it was the hard toil that killed her. The old man raised me by himself. Then, when I was about eighteen summers, he died. That was very sad.'

'Yes, grief can be a strong emotion.'

'Grief had got nothing to do with it. I was sad because he was poor.'

Lang didn't know how to react to such a statement.

'Yeah,' Crawford went on. 'Didn't even own our diddly-squat farmhouse.'

'OK. You'd best start off working on the seam.'

And for the rest of the day Crawford got to know the ropes, helping Rodrigo in the adit.

That evening after supper they were sitting around

the campfire.

'How come nobody ever come across this place before?' Crawford asked.

'They don't now but they did. There are signs near the entrance of the adit that a seam had been worked there many years ago, but it had been exhausted. On the other hand, the source of the placer mining is an underground stream. Way inside the rock there's a small cave where the water appears briefly and then disappears down an abyss. God knows where it comes out, if it ever does. So it never saw the light of day. Any casual passers-by wouldn't have seen it.'

'How did you find it?'

'From the chemical make-up of the rocks I knew there was a possibility hereabouts. I investigated and eventually found the hidden stream. When I'd analysed it and found it contained gold particles, I rechannelled the flow so that it emptied outside and built the sluice box to catch it.'

'How did you rechannel it?'

'Not easily! Cut a channel through to the exterior then dammed the stream at the point where it disappeared into the chasm so that it was diverted to where it could be of use.'

'And the sluice box? How did you get that and all the rest of the stuff out here? You can't get a wagon through those passes.'

'Didn't have to. Brought tools.' He pointed to the

clumps of trees that dotted the darkening landscape. 'As you may have noticed, there's ample timber. Meant a lot of hard work but it got done. And talking about work, time to hit the hay. Work tomorrow. Can't leave it all to our Mexican friends.'

After a morning working at the face Crawford was rinsing off the dust ready for lunch when Lang joined him at the tub.

'How did it go?'

'Like you said, hard work. But I can cope.'

'When you've got into the swing of it, you can alternate working on the sluice.'

Crawford rubbed himself with a towel. 'You'll understand, Grover, I'm still full of questions.'

'Of course you are. We go back long enough for there to be no secrets between us.'

He continued once they were settled round the fire, eating. 'So what do you want to know?'

'Well, for a start, this ain't the kind of place a guy just stumbles on. How did you find it?'

'I didn't exactly find it. I refound it.'

Crawford took a bite of steaming tortilla. 'You are gonna tell an old friend what that means?'

Lang smiled. 'I came across a reference to it in an old text. How the Spaniards originally found the lode is a mystery. Maybe through the Indians, I guess. Anyways, they set up a mine hereabouts, called it the mine of Santa Maria. But, according to the records, they exhausted it after about a year or so.'

'So how come nobody else had tried to work it since?'

'For a start, there's no map giving its location and, to my knowledge, the only reference to it is the one I came across. Then, if anyone did stumble on the information, they probably wouldn't have thought it was worth investing resources into searching for it, as it had been exhausted. Neither was its location described with any clarity.'

'Well, if there's no map, how come you made it here?'

'Going back to my training again. I could use my knowledge of geological formation to have a good guess at its location from clues given in the old text.'

'Maybe, but still a hell of a long shot given that as far as you knew it had been exhausted. When did you come?'

'Nigh on three years back. That was after my stint with you in Montana and a season combing Colorado.'

'How did you get your gear out here originally?'

'I organized the whole thing back in town. Loaded up the burros a couple at a time. Took a long time to get established. Got a sight easier when I took on the Mexicans. As you see, we're housed in tents. Not very bulky when folded so they didn't take up much room on the animals. With long intervals each of the men would lead his two burros to a designated point some way within Deadman's Pass. Took the same precautions I did with you when we came out. When we had all eventually congregated at the point we stayed a while, just to make sure we hadn't aroused anybody's curiosity back in town.'

Crawford looked around the valley. 'And you've lasted here some years? Even with a string of burros you couldn't have brought all your requirements.'

'You're right. We don't have to haul it all in. As you are aware, we have adequate water. Here in the valley the soil is fertile, so we have managed to grow a few vegetables. As for meat, there is a reasonable amount of game. Luxuries – cigars, coffee, the odd pot or pan – I bring them back from town on my visits. So we are now largely self-sufficient.'

'The town. That's another thing. With these regular visits to town how come nobody there has been interested to see where you're getting the gold from?'

'I've told you. I don't use the assayer in town so nobody there knows about the gold. I catch the train to the next place along the line and do my dealing there. On my return I make a note of anybody who gets off the train at the same time and I keep a watch on them until I'm sure nobody's followed me from the assayer before I complete my journey here.'

'You've got it all worked out.'

'Probably not all.'

12

A week passed and Crawford had become a regular member of the crew. One day he was using a scoop to bag an amount of gold dust when Lang joined him.

The younger man glanced to check he was not being overheard. 'I been watching them. You trust them?'

'The Mexes?' Lang said with a smile. 'We all trust each other.'

'I'd never trust a man with something like this and there are *three* of them. You wanna watch yourself. Any time it'd have been no trouble for the three of them to gang up on you. Even now they could kill you, me, drop our bodies down one of the chasms or over a cliff and nobody would ever know.'

Lang smiled at the very idea. 'They're men of principle.'

'I'm still gonna keep my eye on 'em.'

'No need. As I said, they have principles. That's why they have to keep away from Mexico for a time. Their principles clash with those in power. I trust them in the same way they trust me to take their share to the assayers and bring specie back to them.'

'That's another thing. When you go off on your trips, how do you know they're not hiding stuff away back here?'

'It's a long story, but they once trusted me with their lives. The upshot is I would trust them with my well-being, not to mention any of my material possessions.'

Crawford tied the drawstring of the bag. 'So, how long is this idyll gonna last?'

'I reckon at least another year. It is the way of things that an exhaustion point will be reached some time. I've looked around and there is no sign of another seam, at least not in the locality. Nor will the yield from the stream go on for ever.'

'What happens then?'

'I'll have made enough to last me into the foreseeable future. To boot, enough to finance any more exploration further afield, should I get round to it.'

'And the Mexes?'

'The time period suits them. By the time there's nothing left here, they figure the heat will be off them back home and they can return. Plus they'll be taking back a nice little grubstake to keep them going for a spell. As they're active Republicans I reckon they'll still want to change their government down there. Just like we did up here. Don't quite know what specifically they got against the king but their politics is their business.'

The next day Crawford was taking a break with a cigarette when he spotted movement at the end of the valley. Figures!

He quickly located his gunbelt and ran to the mouth of the mine. 'Grover! We got visitors!'

Then, with his Colt levelled, he slowly descended the grade. He could make out four shapes and as they neared he could make out Indians.

'Put your gun away,' Lang shouted as he moved into the sunlight. 'They're friendly. Local Pima.'

'I thought nobody knew about this place?'

'I meant white men who might cause trouble.'

'Where have they come from?' Crawford asked when the older man joined him.

Lang pointed into the distance. 'They climb down the precipice.'

'Precipice? You said there was only one way into the valley.'

'Effectively there is only the one way, the way we came. There's not many with the skill to descend that precipice. It's practically a vertical drop.'

'What they can do, somebody else can do.'

'I don't think so. Beyond the escarpment there is nothing for God knows how many miles. Just untold miles of sun-baked nothingness. There is no reason for anyone to venture across such a wilderness and hence it is highly unlikely that anyone will stumble upon the valley from that end. Even more unlikely they would accidentally hit on the one place where a descent may be made.'

'Hail, Grey Antelope,' Lang called as they neared. The Indian responded and the two continued to exchange ritualized greetings before the leader signalled to two of his men who were carrying a deer to lay it on the grass. Lang responded by going to his tent and returning with the three boxes of cigars.

The chief opened a box, took out a cigar and sniffed along its length, displaying satisfaction. He went to the campfire and, as he and his followers occupied themselves with lighting up and savouring the smokes, Lang turned to Crawford.

'They don't bother us,' he explained in a whisper, 'and we don't bother them. Every now and again we trade, like today, and that's it.'

'They speak English,' the young man observed.

'They're natives, not savages. Grey Antelope spent some time in a missionary school as a child. Don't worry. They stay and talk. They spin it out a bit; some kind of tribal etiquette.'

The Mexicans returned to their tasks while the

visitors stayed for an hour chatting with Lang round the fire. Eventually the Indians rose, indicating their intention to leave.

'Stay one more moment,' Lang said. 'I was forgetting. I have another gift for you.'

He went to his tent and returned with a couple of packages. He handed the larger one to the leader, who unwrapped it to reveal the rifle Lang had bought in town.

'You know how to fire a long arm?'

'I have fired one,' the Indian said, pride in eyes as he examined it, 'but have never owned such a thing.'

'It's a Wesson. You know how to load it?'

'Lang jests.'

The white man passed across the remaining package containing several boxes of ammunition. 'You'll need these.'

Grey Antelope wielded the weapon as though it conferred some special status.

'It shoots well,' Lang said. 'I've tested it. It will be a considerable aid to your hunting. It's especially made for long distance. And there's enough shells there to keep you going for some time.'

Grey Antelope gripped the white man's forearm. 'Lang is a brother.'

And with that the Pima visitors loped back along the valley, disappearing as quickly and as quietly as they had first appeared.

13

It was a month on. Lang was packing little bags of gold dust into his saddle-bags in preparation for one of his trips through the rocky labyrinth. The yield was good and all was right with the world.

Crawford appeared at his side. 'I'd like to come with you.'

'Admirable. That way we can bring back a few extra supplies.'

'No, Grover. I mean I don't want to come back. Truth is I'm getting cabin fever.'

Despite the fact that he could breathe more free air than a man could handle, and had nothing but the wide heavens above while the canyon was so huge that he could hardly see to the end, he felt cooped up.

Lang paused in his task. 'Listen, you're on a good thing here, Monte,' he said, patting the bags and indicating with a thumb the workings behind him.

'When you've had a short break back in the outside world, you'll think different, I'm sure.'

'No,' Crawford said. Hell, did he miss a drink. Then there was having a good time, cards and women, especially women – all the things that made life worth living. This was no living. 'No, Grover. I need to get out *permanent.*'

Lang looked at him. With his own compulsions driving him, it hadn't occurred to him that the life might not appeal to all men. He nodded as he mulled it over. He had to admit he had noticed some tension. There had been snappy exchanges between the young man and his fellow workers.

'What about those guys who are after you out there? You know they're the reason why you wanted to hide away in the first place.'

'I've been out here long enough for my trail to have gone cold. Even if they ever hit on Apache Flats, they'll be long gone now. Fact is, staying here has met its purpose for me and I'm obliged for you giving me the opportunity. That's all I wanted out of it.'

Lang breathed deep. 'OK, Monte, if you've made up your mind.'

He continued packing the bags. 'And you won't have to cool your heels waiting for me to translate this stuff into hard cash over in Dana. I've got enough funds back home in Apache Flats to pay you your due for the work you've done here.'

101

'That's appreciated, Grover.'

Lang winked. 'And enough to give my old pal a leaving bonus.'

Back in Apache Flats Lang watched his little nephew toddling around the kitchen as Juanita prepared lunch.

The two men had returned from the Santa Maria the previous evening. Crawford had stayed overnight and left early that morning.

Lang smiled at Jimmy's antics with a potato rolling around the floor. 'Boy, has he grown in a month.'

'*Sí*,' Juanita said. 'A month is a long time at his age.'

'You know, it hurts me that Jim is not around to see his son as he shoots up like this. A kid makes you see the world afresh, with the eyes of a child. Jim is missing all that.'

She put down the knife she was using for cutting vegetables and crossed the room to put her arms around him. 'It hurts me too, *señor*, but what has happened has happened.'

'They say time heals all wounds but, you know, I doubt it. Some things you don't forget. In particular it makes me feel guilty that I'm here to enjoy the things he'll never see.'

'Do you have faith, *señor*?'

'I go to church on Sundays.'

'Well, if you are a true believer you will know that Jim is up there looking down, *señor*. And he is happy to see you gain pleasure in his child. And it will give him comfort that his son's needs are being met by a loving guardian such yourself.'

Lang gripped her arm in response and they stayed that way before she eventually returned to her task.

'I am glad your Monte Crawford has gone,' she said, changing the mood as she scooped the vegetables into a pot. 'I know he is your friend, *señor*, but now he has gone, I can be frank and say I did not like the man.'

'I admit he was getting tiresome. It was becoming plain he was not suited to the work out there.' Lang chuckled. 'Fact is, I don't think he is suited to work – period. He's a rolling stone and always looking for the quick buck. He liked the money he earned at the mine – I could see it in his eyes when I paid him off – but he didn't cotton to what he had to do to get it.'

She busied herself for a moment then said, 'There was something about him.'

'He's quite a character, all right. I'll admit that. He didn't say but I got the feeling he only joined the army to get away from something. Like someone was after him. Just like when he turned up here looking for a hideaway a month ago. I didn't tell you about that but he was on the run. Some nasty business over in New Mexico. God knows whatever the things are that he gets involved in. Another thing; I never told you, but in the prison camp he was hornswoggling all the time, always managing to get his hands on rare supplies and trading them. Yeah, he's a wily critter all right. But deep down I guess he's a good sort really.'

'I don't know about that. I just can't see it. I do know he didn't like me.'

'Is that so? You felt it even in the short time that you met him? I never noticed it.'

'A woman can tell. I got the feeling it was because I am Mexican.'

'Maybe. Now that you mention it, he wasn't the best of friends with Miguel and the other guys out there. I accepted that it was cabin fever like he said, but there may have been more behind it. Well, you won't have to worry. We've seen the last of him. I'm no fool; I know him. He was just using me. That's the way he is. But he's gone now.'

Juanita brightened up. 'So, what do you want for a packed lunch when you make your trip to Dana City tomorrow?'

'I'll be happy with anything you make.'

'And then back to the mine?'

He watched her as she busied herself about the kitchen. 'When I get back from Dana, we'll go out to Moonbeam. There's some work I want to do on the place. We can spend the whole day there.'

'That will be nice.'

'Besides, it will give me more time in your company. Fact is, I miss you as well as little Jimmy.'

14

With an animal grunt, Monte Crawford rolled off the woman as soon as he had expended himself. He was so drunk it had been difficult for him to climax. Indeed, it had strained the woman's professional skills to render his body capable of any kind of performance at all.

As he struggled to pull up his pants, he knocked the empty whiskey bottle off the dresser.

'Clumsy bozo,' the woman muttered to the ceiling.

His pants in place, he dropped a bill on the table and staggered towards the door.

The woman shuffled to the edge of the bed and dropped her feet to the bare boards.

The boredom writ large in her features changed to irritation when she saw the money.

'That is not the agreed sum!' she shouted at the disappearing figure.

Pushing forward, he fought to focus his eyes in order to scour the drinking parlour for his friend. 'Come on, Jonesy. Time to get out of this crap hole.'

The man called Jonesy rose and could see the woman over his friend's shoulder. She had reached the door and was leaning against the jamb with her shift only partly covering her body.

'The bastard short-changed me,' she yelled.

Crawford grinned and continued his stagger to the outer door. 'Women!'

'You hear, Rico?' the woman went on. 'The bastard's left owing.'

The bartender, a giant of a man, looked perplexed. A short, wiry man came from a back room, looked at the one behind the counter and pointed to the door. 'Somebody needs teaching a lesson. And give me your baseball bat.'

Out on the boardwalk Crawford straightened his clothing. 'Time to hit the hay. What do you think, Jonesy?'

His friend didn't have time to reply as a voice rasping, 'And where do you think you're going?' cut the night air.

They turned to see two figures silhouetted against the light spilling out through the doorway: the one the woman had called Rico and behind him the bartender.

'And what's it got to do with you?' Crawford slurred.

'You short-change my woman, you short-change me, the one called Rico said.

'Huh, she wasn't worth what I did pay her,' Crawford said with a grin.

'Now that's what I call adding insult to injury,' the little man said. 'Requires additional compensation.'

'Additional compensation?' Crawford said, making some effort in his drunken way to mimic the reedy voice.

The little man put his hand out at his side and, without instruction, the bartender slipped the bat into it.

Attempting to throw a grin at his now apprehensive friend, Crawford didn't see the weapon coming. It caught him on the side of the head and sent him sprawling backwards. Almost simultaneously the bulky bartender put a hammer fist into Jonesy's stomach that doubled him up so that as his chin went down it met another meaty fist coming up.

The saloon men obviously relished the chance to seek retribution and continued to rain down shattering blows until it was plain that the fallen men were no longer feeling anything.

They went through the pockets of the unconscious casualties.

'As I thought,' Rico said when they'd finished. 'Shithead drifters, no more than a few dollars and cents between them.'

'Not the kind of bindle-stiffs we want in our town, would you say, boss?' the bartender said.

Rico handed the money to the woman who had come to the door to watch the spectacle.

'I should say not,' she said. 'Couldn't even get it up right.'

She sashayed close and put her arm through that of her little man. 'Not like my Rico,' she purred. 'Throw the scumbags over their horses and dump 'em out of town. You know how to deal with them if they come back.'

The cry of a killdeer was breaking the morning silence as the 'scumbags' came to.

Jonesy was the first to open his eyes. He groaned, putting his hand to his stomach then gingerly felt his face. He hauled himself to a sitting position and the first thing he saw was their horses some distance away, grazing nonchalantly as though nothing had happened. He groaned and twisted his head slowly to take stock of their surroundings. He'd just sighted the town a few hundred yards on when he heard his companion moaning into wakefulness.

He studied the lumps and blood-caked features of his companion as the eyes flickered.

'Jeez, if I look as bad as you, I must look a sight,' he concluded.

From his prone position Monte Crawford focused with some effort on his friend. 'You do.'

'But you look really bad, Monte.'

Crawford's fingers tenderly explored the bat-inflicted protuberances that had somewhat rearranged the geography of his face. 'Jeez, I must do. If I had more than a handful of dollars, I'd see a doc.'

They hauled themselves to their feet. When they had staggered across the sand to reclaim their horses they discovered the animals had sensibly parked themselves near a stream.

The two men drank and cleaned themselves.

As they sat reflecting on the ways of the world, Jonesy suddenly noticed his pockets were empty. 'Hey, the bastards took my money. And I didn't even cause the trouble.'

The observation prompted the other to check his own pockets. 'Damn! Same here. Not a dime.'

They sat silently for a spell.

'What now, Monte?'

'Well, we ain't going back there, that's for sure. We need money not trouble.'

Half an hour on they were ambling along, slumped over their saddle horns, not knowing where they were headed save for the knowledge they were not headed for the scene of the previous night's débâcle.

'Where are Nathan and Russ holed up these days?' Crawford said out of the blue.

Jonesy pondered, then said, 'Fort Leonard, last I heard.'

Crawford put some thought into it. 'Fort Leonard? That means they're reachable from here, don't it?'

'Yeah, with some riding. Why them?'

'Got an idea. Four men should be able to pull it off.'

'Pull what off?'

'Big bucks! Enough dinero to put us in clover for hell of a spell.' He put some more thought into it. 'Yes, all it needs is four men who can handle themselves and ain't a-feared of pulling a trigger.'

'Big bucks? Hell, Monte, we ain't got a bill to wipe our ass on at the moment. Our main problem is how to get food inside us.'

'Hey, my pessimistic friend, those punchy whorehouse yasser-bosses didn't take everything. They left us with our horses and guns, didn't they? There'll be enough dry-goods and grocery stores between here and Fort Leonard to provide cash for basics.'

'I don't know that, Monte. Don't cotton to knocking over small-time stores. That's how a guy can end up in the slammer – just for dimes. And I don't want the slammer again, you know that.'

'That's the point about crummy little jobs, Mr Jones. Small towns, small takes – nobody's gonna send a posse out for a few nickels. And all we need is enough to get us by for a week or two till I get this job going.'

15

Four horsemen were working their way slowly across the sand, having long left the trail out of Apache Flats. The leading rider, lumpy bruising on his face still showing, was perpetually scanning the environment. Unlike the men to his rear he was unconcerned with the heat and flies; his mind was concentrated on some task.

'There it is,' Monte Crawford suddenly said, pointing to a cottonwood. 'That's where I tethered my horse while I was waiting for Lang.'

'Huh,' Nathan, one of his new recruits, said. 'One cottonwood looks the same to me.'

'No,' Crawford countered. 'This is the one all right. I sat here long enough while I waited for him. Now, from here on we kept to the plain riding parallel with the rocky terrain to the west. Then we turned sharply.'

On the journey to Fort Leonard he and Jonesy

had picked up enough cash via minor robberies to meet their immediate needs, together with some to cover basic supplies for the forthcoming expedition. They had succeeded in finding their two buddies and had talked them into joining the venture. Strictly, they had only had to persuade old-timer Nathan. The young Russ went along with anything his sidekick said and, in keeping with his 'tag-along' character, now took up the rear.

As they proceeded Crawford studied the deep fissures that split the rocky outcrops, looking for the way in. 'There,' he shouted, 'that's the one, the gateway!'

The other riders followed him over the shale. Eventually they were standing on the last high bench of a rise and facing the entrance of a narrow canyon.

'Are you sure?' Nathan asked. 'Ain't much to choose between any of the cracks we been riding past in the last half an hour.'

'I've told you,' Crawford snapped. 'I've been this way twice already. First time it was all new and maybe I didn't take much stock. But when I came back I was deliberately keeping a note up here.' He tapped his head. 'This is it, believe me.'

They eased their way single file between the cramped, unyielding sides of the rocky fracture. Some thirty yards further ahead the gully took a tight bend, and as they eased around the corner in the rock, a blast of sunlight shafted through to dazzle them.

Shielding his eyes, Crawford paused while he considered the route ahead. He recognized where the gully widened, the high cliffs giving way to gentler flanking slopes studded with cacti, boulders and thorny brush.

'Yeah, we're on the right track,' he said as he nudged his horse. Further on, as he had expected, the sidewalls closed in again, the gully mouth shrinking to a gap just wide enough for the column riders to pass in single file.

Crawford was finding the going gruelling but straightforward. However, by noon he was beginning to have doubts. By then they had worked their way through countless intersecting canyons and at each one he had had to make a choice. And he met the repeated grumblings of his fellow travellers with an increasingly feigned certainty.

'When do we rest, Monte?' Jonesy asked. He looked around at his companions. 'We're all bushed.'

'OK,' Crawford said. 'We'll noon here. But we can't stay long. We gotta make a certain spot where we can camp for the night.' He waved a hand at the daunting rock faces that surrounded them, each one acting like a mirror to the unforgiving sun. 'Until then it's all gonna look like this. The place we're aiming for is a perfect site. It's out of the sun, sheltered by oak trees, and there's running water. It'll provide just the location for us to recover our strength in preparation for the last leg.'

Come afternoon they took another rest. They were about to remount when there was a scream from the young Russ. He had been urinating against a canyon wall a few feet from the main group. When they got to him he was gripping his leg. 'Rattler! Rattler!'

A faint rattle could still be heard as the snake worked its way back into the safety of a rocky crack.

'What can you do?' the kid shouted. 'What can you do?'

None of them dared to say, 'Nothing'. They just looked at each other. 'Where did it get you, kid?' Crawford asked.

'Near the knee.'

Crawford pulled his knife and slit the lad's pants. The purple fang marks were quite visible and the surrounding tissue already ballooning.

He untied the bandanna from round his neck and tied a tourniquet above the knee. 'That should stop the flow of poison, kid.'

He stepped back and spoke to Nathan in a whispered tone. 'Can we cut out the poison?'

'Don't think it would help. Reckon it's spreading as we speak.'

'I've heard amputation can work,' Jonesy put in.

'Hell, man,' Crawford hissed. 'We're not in a goddamn hospital.'

He grunted in frustration, went to his horse and took a bottle of whiskey from his saddle-bag. He removed the makeshift dressing from the leg of the groaning youngster and poured some of the amber liquid over the ugly holes before he reapplied the bandanna.

Then he handed the bottle to the stricken lad. 'We're going for help. Sink some of this while we're gone. It might help.'

He winked at the other men and they rode off the way they had come. When they were out of sight Crawford signed for them to rein in.

'Reckon it'll take ten minutes at the most.'

In due time they returned to find his estimate had been about right. They contemplated the frozen contorted face.

'He was only a kid,' the wizened-faced Nathan said, 'But we rode a few trails together.'

'In that case you're the one to say something over him,' Crawford said. He retrieved his bottle which had fallen from the dead man's hand, and took a swig before returning it to his saddle-bag.

Nathan muttered a few words. Then he said, 'Reckon that's it,' as he began helping himself to Russ's canteen, food and other valuables. 'The job's off.'

'No it ain't,' Crawford said. 'We press on.'

'Don't be crazy. Three against four? Ain't gonna work, Monte.'

'Where's your guts, man? They're simple workmen out there. An old man and three peasants who now think they're miners. Ain't used to confrontations with guns. It's meat and drink to us. Just as important, we'll have the drop on 'em.'

'You said Lang was an army man.'

'Did I – hell! He served as an engineer. Reckon he's never fired a gun. He won't offer much resistance.'

He mounted up and made do with a single glance back to check the others were following him.

With light fading fast they turned a bend to find themselves at yet another confluence of cross-cutting canyons with ragged rims towering over the intruders.

Crawford dropped from his horse and contemplated the intimidating scene.

'Now which way?' Jonesy asked.

'This ain't the paradise you spoke of a ways back,' Nathan said, in response to Crawford's silence. 'No babbling brook, no trees. In fact we ain't seen flowing water since noon. Good job we still got some in our canteens.'

'It's gonna be dark soon,' Crawford said eventually, trying to maintain some optimism in his voice. 'We'll bivouac here for the night.'

*

Come morning Crawford was up first, exploring the various fissures and canyon entrances.

'Don't know what you're doing that for?' Nathan said when he got back. 'We're retracing our steps before our brains fry.'

'We're not going back now.'

'Monte, this is a hell-and-gone-back place,' Jonesy said. 'Old Nathan's right.'

'I'm boss on this caper,' Crawford said. 'We're going on.'

'If you're going on, Monte, you're going by yourself. This job's turned into a bum steer. I thought it was nuts when you suggested it but I went along with it for old times' sake. But there's a limit and we've crossed it.'

Crawford pointed to one of the vertical cracks. 'That's the way, I'm sure. We didn't make the stream by nightfall because we were travelling slower than before. And we were delayed by that business with Russ. But that's the way all right.'

'Hog swill,' Nathan said. 'You ain't got any more idea than we have. We're going back. While you were gallivanting out there doing your exploring we had a vote.'

Crawford eyed the men in turn. 'You too, Jonesy?'

'Nathan's right, Monte. We gotta give our priority to simple survival now. Otherwise we'll end up like Russ.'

Crawford looked at the ground while he thought.

'OK,' he conceded. 'Two against one swings it. Ain't no point me going on by myself.'

He didn't say but in reality he felt he'd already taken a wrong turn somewhere back aways. It had already been dawning on him that, when they'd eventually called a halt the previous night, they probably weren't anywhere near the Santa Maria. But a leader sometimes doesn't like to admit he's wrong.

They had more confidence on their return trip. Each having experienced the trip to that point, each could make some contribution to selecting the right route. One would remember some natural feature, another would note scuffmarks.

However, when they didn't come across their former companion's body when expected, they realized that despite their combined knowledge they had taken a wrong turn.

They retraced their most recent tracks and made another choice at one of the junctions. That it was the right choice was confirmed when they eventually passed Russ's sad remains. But the detour meant they had lost a lot of time, so that it began to get dark a lot sooner than they had hoped.

They were short on water and their food was used up but when they bedded down for the night near some seemingly familiar piñon trees, their worries lessened. They recognized where they were and

120

reckoned a couple of hours in the morning would
see them out in the open.

16

Grover Lang increasingly enjoyed the company of his sister-in-law. In time they became closer. He extended his stays at home during his trips out from the Santa Maria and would always bring her a present from Dana City.

On such occasions, when little Jimmy was tucked up in bed, they would sit before the fire and Lang would help her improve her English with a primer. They played cards and she proved a worthy opponent, especially when they played Mexican games that she explained to him. He had a piano – he had played occasionally since his college days – and when she told him she liked singing he ordered some sheet music of Mexican songs from Chicago and they performed together, with Little Jimmy providing a delighted audience.

Time and time again on such occasions a question rose in his mind but his awkwardness in such matters always held him back.

Meanwhile the house of Moonbeams was almost ready for them to move in.

Seemed that nothing could disturb the cosiness of the Lang household.

Calor was an end-of-road town. The derelict diggings just out of town were all that remained of the original reason why folk had trekked out to the middle of nowhere and set up a huddle of shacks that didn't merit the name of 'town'. Whatever ore had been there in the first place was quickly exhausted and the bulk of hardnosed prospectors had moved on to the next place where there was some whisper of rich pickings. As they had come that far, the less energetic hopefuls had stayed on, resigning themselves to an attempt to tame the wilderness. But their stubbornness went unrewarded. The inhospitability of the plateau, its alkaline soil and flatness that offered no protection against winds, all combined to deny life to anything planted, with the result that each year marked a further declining population.

The place had the smell of abandonment but that was what Monte Crawford liked about the town: a virtual ghost town would have no law officer. That meant no wanted posters on a notice board to make things awkward.

The four men stopped outside a tumbledown

shack labelled 'Saloon', its open door hanging by one remaining hinge. Crawford contemplated the plain shimmering to the horizon, then headed past the door into the welcome shade.

After purchasing drinks, he turned and chopped his arm back towards the doorway. 'Believe there's a canyon yonder.'

The bartender looked in the indicated direction, then returned to stacking glasses. 'Heard tell. Marks the end of the plateau. Way beyond the horizon, and then some. Never been that way myself. Fact, no cause for *anybody* to go there.'

'If a guy wanted to get down into the canyon, say as a short cut, you know of a way down?'

The man laughed. 'Short cut! That's a short cut to nowheres, saving hell!'

'So you don't know of a path down?' Crawford persisted.

'Sure ain't no path that I know of. It's a sheer drop from what I hear, man. If there's a way down only God knows it. And maybe an old Indian or two.'

Crawford bought more drinks and the four took their glasses outside. He leant on the hitch rail and peered across the bleached landscape. 'The guy back there said maybe Indians know the way to the valley floor. He wasn't sure but I *know* that some Indians know. When I was at the Santa Maria we were visited by Indians and Grover said they had

124

climbed down the precipice.'

Nathan looked apprehensively across the heat-hazed plain. 'Indians?'

'Don't worry. Friendly Indians. They knew of a way into the valley. Grover said there's not many with the skill to descend the precipice. Made him feel safe. Said it was highly unlikely that anyone would stumble upon the valley. But what those Indians can do, we can do.'

He slung the liquor to the back of his throat. 'We'll take one more drink and then go take a look-see for ourselves.'

They peered over the edge. 'Well, the barman was right about one thing. It's sheer cliff. Makes a guy dizzy just contemplating it.'

Jonesy stepped back, awe written large in his features. 'Let's go back, boss. This is another bum deal. This place has got nothing to offer but death and bad times.'

'There's gold for the taking out there,' Crawford said, looking into the void. 'A prize like that's never easy.' He looked along the bleached rock of the perimeter one way, then the other. 'We ain't crossed that alkali wasteland to turn back without some investigation.'

'The barkeep said there was no way down.' The speaker was Case, Nathan's brother. Having just come out of prison and being broke he had been a natural replacement for the snake-bit Russ.

'And he also said he'd never been out here,' Crawford rejoined. 'That means he knows zilch. May as well do a little more exploring now we've got this far.'

He nodded at Nathan and his brother, and pointed east. 'You guys, explore the edge that way. Me and Jonesy will go the other. We'll meet back here in two hours.'

'Two hours?' Case said. 'Christ, out here in this heat?'

'Yeah. I figure a good walking speed will mean we'll have checked about four miles of the rim between us. And not wasted all of our time. OK, you know what we're looking for: some means of descent. Now git.'

It was late afternoon when the four exhausted men met up again, none having discovered anything that showed promise.

'What do we do next, boss?' Jonesy wanted know.

'We don't give up, that's for sure. There's a way down. The Indians know it. They been here since time immemorial. Ain't nothing they don't know.'

He looked at the setting sun. 'But we can't do much more today. Let's get back to town before the sun disappears altogether. We can all do with a rest and sleep.'

*

The next day the four sauntered into the saloon.

As Crawford ordered drinks he gazed around the room. A couple of old-timers were debating some point. His eyes lingered on an Indian slumped on a seat in a corner.

The bartender saw the look. 'Trust you don't mind him, pal,' he said as he poured the drinks. 'I know a lotta bars don't allows Injuns in. Smell the place up.'

Crawford agreed but he wasn't looking for an argument. 'Makes no never-mind to me.'

'As long as a body has got the spending stuff,' the bartender continued, 'he's welcome.' He looked up from his task and across at the Indian. 'Well, maybe I don't exactly lay out the welcome mat, but I'll take his dollars.'

Crawford swigged back the drink. His mind was elsewhere.

'Yeah, he's something of a scoundrel,' the barman continued.

'Scoundrel?' Crawford echoed half-heartedly.

'Yeah. A Pima, ostracized by his tribe. They'll have nothing to do with him. Contravened some tribal code.'

Crawford's ears pricked up. 'You mean he's a loner?'

'Does odd jobs to get his drinking money. He's in

a vicious circle. Nothing he does, do his people like. His drunkenness stains the tribal honour apparently. And they don't cotton to his lackeying for whites.'

'He knows the locality?'

'Been around these parts as long I can remember.'

'What's his name?'

'Don't know his Pima name. We call him Blackjack.'

Half an hour later the four visitors were sitting outside the saloon, backs against the wall, when the Indian stepped out into the sunlight.

Crawford gestured for him to join them.

'They tell me your name's Blackjack.'

The man nodded.

'Mine's Crawford.' He pointed into the wilderness. 'I hear there's a canyon out there.'

'Yes. Long way.'

'You know it?'

The Indian nodded.

'You know a way down into the canyon?'

'There is no reason to go.'

'I have a reason to go. And I can give you a reason to go.'

'I not understand.'

'Money to show us how to get down.'

'How much?'

'That's better.' He thumbed at the saloon door. 'Mr Jones, be so good as to fetch us some more drinks. Me and Mr Blackjack have got some talking to do.'

17

Miguel was mending the woven-ocotillo pen in which they kept the horse and mules. There must have been a windstorm during the night. Nobody had been aware of it but the residents of the Santa Maria had woken to a sandy taste in the air, while a reddish film over the area was detectable. And a section of the animal pen was down.

Lang and Miguel were busy with saws building an extension to the sluice box while the smell of Felipe's cooking wafted over the valley.

The faint sounds of their labours was all that could be heard.

That was until a shot rang out causing them all to halt in their tasks and look about in bewilderment. Their eyes raked all around the valley for the source.

'Don't nobody move!' some unseen person bellowed.

And then Lang saw a figure, with rifle levelled at the shoulder, break cover on the opposite slope and start to descend. Then another, similarly threatening with a rifle, was advancing along the valley floor.

Felipe dropped a skillet and started to run towards his tent where he kept his gun. There was another explosion and the Mexican pitched forward, rolled and lay inert.

'Put your hands up, all of you,' the original shouter went on. 'Walk slowly into the open at the bottom of the valley.'

The two workers threw glances at each other and did as they were bid. Neither of them was armed and they had no idea how many attackers there were. By the time they had congregated in the dip they could see that there were four intruders.

Then Lang recognized Crawford. 'You're a man of dark intent, Monte.'

'We don't want to hurt nobody, Grover,' Crawford said as he drew near. 'It was unfortunate about the Mexican there – but he had been warned. Jonesy, there's another greaser somewhere.' He pointed to the adit. 'He usually works in the cave.'

Jonesy cautiously ascended the grade, gun aimed at the opening. He'd taken cover at the side when Rodrigo came out of the darkness, covered in dust, wielding a hammer.

'Get wise, feller,' Jonesy said. 'Ain't worth getting

hurt for. Drop the hammer.'

'Do as he says, Rodrigo,' Lang shouted.

The Mexican let the hammer fall and allowed himself to be ushered down the grade.

Lang turned back to Crawford. 'What do you want, Monte?'

'We're gonna tie you up.' He pointed to the niche in the rocks. 'Case, that's their store – the hole in the wall. You'll find adequate rope in there.'

He looked back at Lang. 'First you tell us where the Mexicans stash their wages. It'll amount to quite a fortune by now. And then, of course, the gold dust in the present consignment that you're building up.'

'And if we don't tell you where any of it is?'

'I don't want to cause you any physical harm, Grover. But my *compadres* are not so considerate. It won't mean anything to them to wipe you all out. Then we can find what we want for ourselves. So it will be easier on you and your boys if you co-operate.'

'They say a bad penny will always turn up at some time, Monte.'

Some unspoken communication passed between the remaining two Mexicans. Then Miguel said, 'We have worked hard and long for what we've got, Señor Lang. We do not see that we should part with it for the asking.'

Case moved forward and levered his rifle butt into the face of the miner, knocking him senseless to the ground. He stood triumphantly over the still form and rested the end of his gun barrel on the man's unconscious head.

'If they don't tell us what we want to know we'll just kill 'em one by one. Starting with this greaser.'

'No need to be too hasty, Case,' Crawford said. 'I figure our friends are changing their minds already.'

Lang cursed to himself. This was such an off-the-map place it had never occurred to him to post guards.

'You wouldn't let your boys wreak mayhem, would you, Monte?' he said. 'You ain't that bloodthirsty.'

Case replied for his boss. 'Ain't no never-mind to me, mister. Next shot I kill this shithead. Then one by one. I'm used to getting what I want.'

He histrionically changed the angle of his gun against Miguel's head. 'The count starts now. One, two. . . .'

There was an echoing crack and the man with the ominously poised gun twisted in a muscular spasm, fell face down and slithered down the screed of the slight dip beside which he had been standing, a hole in the side of his head.

The remaining three no-goods spun round, eyes raking the canyon, but, just as had happened with their own gunfire, the reverberating sound against the rock walls was making it difficult to locate the source. Crawford dived for cover and, when another shot put Jonesy down, he could see Indians advancing along the gully floor. But they were mere dots. How the hell could they be accurate from that distance?

For seconds there was confusion.

At the bottom of the adit grade, Rodrigo bent down and claimed Jonesy's gun, bringing it up into a firing position.

'Let's get the hell out of here, Nathan,' Crawford shouted.

But Nathan never had a chance to put the instruction into effect, a neat shot from Rodrigo went clear through his throat; arterial blood fountained from his neck.

Lang dashed to the shack. When he emerged with a rifle he could make out Crawford scrabbling upwards across the rocky terrain, the crest of which marked the entrance to the canyon.

'He dropped his gun, *señor*,' Rodrigo shouted, pointing.

Lang worked his way down and picked up the gang leader's fallen weapon. He pushed it into his belt and swung his eyes up to the ridge over which Crawford had now disappeared.

He checked that the three men were dead. Then he turned to face the approaching Indians and raised a flat hand in welcome.

The gesture was reciprocated by the leading

Indian, who brandished the long-barrelled Wesson and grinned. 'Grover glad he gave me gift?' he shouted.

'Yeah,' Lang said, 'but it never occurred to me that it would be used for its present purpose.'

The Indian signed to one of his men and gestured to Crawford's escape route. The man broke into a determined run after the gang leader.

'Hold,' Lang shouted.

'Why?' the leader asked.

'He was a friend,' Lang explained. 'Did me a favour once.'

The Indian grunted his lack of understanding. 'If he is friend, *señor*, what kind of enemies do you have?' He yelled something in Pima and the pursuing Indian halted in his lope and began to return.

Lang looked around. 'Save for that one, you get them all?'

'Yes. We followed them. Counted four.'

Lang stepped forward and clenched the man's arm. 'Well, I'm glad you chanced to turn up when you did.' He looked along the length of the canyon and added with a dry chuckle, 'Figure it bamboozled 'em how they could be attacked with a rifle from such a distance.

Noting that Miguel was staggering but mobile, he moved over to where Rodrigo was examining Felipe. 'How is he?'

'He's coming round, *señor*.'

After the Mexican had pulled off his shirt to serve as a cushion for his friend's head, he stood up. 'If the *señor* tends to Felipe, it will be my pleasure to dispense with the last of the *bastardos*.' He put out his hand for Lang's rifle.

'No, Rodrigo. I reckon he don't know the way out. And he's got no food. Chances are we'll find a pile of bones next time we journey through.'

'Why leave it to Nature, *señor*?'

'For personal reasons I just can't see him killed, Rodrigo. Mind, after what he's perpetrated today, neither will I help him.'

'He could be back, *señor*.'

'With no weapon, he won't be a threat.'

'He could still be back. When he realizes he can't find his way he'll know that returning here will be his only chance.'

'We'll cross that bridge when, or if, we come to it. But you're right, we'll mount a guard. However, like I said, I figure he's no peril to us now.'

His attention returned to the Indian. 'How come you turned up when you did like that?'

'It was not chance. It came to our knowledge that the white renegades had been asking if there was a way down here across the plateau. One of our group, a Pima the whites call Blackjack, he a bad sort. We caught sight of the turncoat returning to the precipice as we journeyed here. The man do

136

anything for a dollar. It was he showed them the way. When we learned of what he intended, we followed.'

Lang gave a smile that radiated relief. 'Glad you did.'

18

It was a warm day in Dana City as Grover Lang walked along the boardwalk. The assault on the Santa Maria was a distant memory. Miguel and Felipe had completely recovered under the care of Juanita.

'If you don't want any trouble do as I say.' It was the voice of someone who had fallen in step alongside him. He turned but didn't recognize the speaker.

'What the—?'

'Just follow me. Otherwise some real nasty things might happen.'

The man crossed the street and entered an alleyway.

Lang followed him and came face to face with Monte Crawford, his bruising now hardly noticeable.

'Surprised to see me, Grover?'

'What's—?'

Before he had finished the question his escort pushed him roughly forward to face the wall, hands hard against the brickwork.

'Get his gun, Matt,' Crawford said.

The man removed Lang's Colt from the leather holster hidden by his black jacket, then ran hands down his sides and legs.

'I'm a businessman, Monte, not a walking armoury.'

'And as a businessman you won't need this,' Crawford said, taking the Colt. He pushed it into his belt. 'Like I said, surprised to see me?' he went on.

Lang turned. 'Must admit, never thought I'd see you again.'

'That's because you thought I was dead, isn't it?'

'That – or because of the two times you double-crossed me.'

Crawford ignored the accusations. 'You thought I was dead because of the state I was in the last time our paths crossed. Got no weapon and heading off into that maze of rock. Yes, I was in a bad way and my old army pal didn't come to check I was OK. Well, *pal*, surprising as it may seem, I finally found my way out of your bloody labyrinth. Yeah, Lady Luck saw fit to shine on me that time. Not like the first time we tried to get to that damn hideaway of yours.'

'Not the first time? You mean you and your

139

desperadoes had already tried to get to the Santa Maria?'

'Yeah. You didn't know about that did you? Tried to reach your place once before but it turned bad and we went astray someplace. Lost one of my pals who took a rattler bite. And we had to make our way back.'

Lang nodded. 'That explains the body we found.'

'Yeah, I made it back, no thanks to you.'

'It was still thanks to me. Luck was obviously on your side for you to make it, but I gave you that chance.'

'Did you hell?'

'When your attack on the Santa Maria failed, it was all I could do to stop the Indians and my Mexican crew from pursuing you into the canyons and finishing you off.'

'So you say.'

'Believe me or not, as you see fit. It makes no never-mind what you think now, but I'll tell you one thing: my ever helping you again ended on that day. I owed a debt to you, sure, and had turned a blind eye to your subsequent double-crossing me. But I don't feel obliged to any more.'

'You're a stand-up-straight man and you know that every breath you take until your dying day you owe to me. Wasn't for me you'd have been fish-bait long ago – and don't you forget it. And that's why you're going to do me another favour.'

'I am? And what's that?'

'You are going to give me every cent in your bank account. For a long time I thought the booty lay in the Santa Maria: the Mex money, the gold dust, the gold yet to be mined. Maybe it still does. But having failed twice to grab it, it occurred to me there was just as much, maybe more, sitting in your bank right here in Dana. And my old pal, whose life I saved, would only be too willing to hand it over. A fortune with no sweating with a pickaxe or sifting through garbage, no breaking our asses hauling the stuff around. A treasure available in simple green spending form.'

'And why should I do that?'

'A token of letting bygones be bygones.'

'Don't be stupid.'

'Yeah, I was funning with that remark. The reason why you're gonna withdraw it and hand it over is because you value your blue-eyed nephew.'

'Jimmy! What's he got to do with anything?'

'Yeah, I've watched you with him. Round the campfire at the mine you talked of little else. Funny that, and it's not even your child. Main thing is, you really think the sun shines out of his little butt.'

The blood had drained from Lang's face on realization of what was being threatened. 'You wouldn't!'

'You're probably right there. You and I go back a spell, so maybe I wouldn't harm him. But my new

141

pals, like the old gang that your Injuns disposed of, ain't so charitable.'

'Where is he?'

'With his momma.'

'But where?'

'They're safe and they'll stay that way as long as you don't cause us any problems.'

'That means you been to the apartment in Apache Flats?'

'Of course.'

'And they're there now?'

'The woman is tied up there. Keeps her out of the way. She's gagged well so she won't be able to raise the alarm if anybody comes a-calling.'

'You haven't hurt her?'

'Don't worry. We got bigger fish to fry.'

'And Jimmy? What have you done with Jimmy?'

'It was better to get him out of town as a safeguard against any complications. When my pal Matt and I followed you on the train here to Dana another pal of mine collected the kid, so that by now he'll be tucked away in a useful hideaway we've found.'

'Where's that?'

'You'll find out soon enough.'

'Tell me where.'

'OK. You'll like this touch, Grover. See, we needed some place where nobody would interfere. Somewhere convenient, out of Apache Flats and not too far from Dana. Then I remembered, back at Santa Maria round the campfire, as well as spouting about the kid you warbled on about just such a place that you were setting up. You gave it the fanciful name of Moonbeam, as I recall.'

Lang hissed at the notion of these hardcases defiling his dream. 'And how did you get him there? Little Jimmy's never been on a horse.'

'No problem. Found a very handy buggy in back of your place. Also it helped to hide the little bugger from prying eyes on the journey. Anyways, your Moonbeam has turned out ideal, and that's where we're going when you've collected the money.'

'If you hurt him. . . .'

'See how my persuasive powers are working already, Matt? Now this is the way we're gonna work it. I aim to keep my face off the streets as much as I can so Matt here will accompany you to the bank. But I'll warn you. A couple of the boys that got shot out at the Santa Maria, Nathan and Case, were two of three brothers, name of Paterson. Well, this is Matt Paterson, the last brother. He's very upset about what happened to his kin and so is his dear little old mother.'

'Their deaths were not my doing.'

'You may not have pulled the trigger but he holds you responsible. So watch your step in your dealings with him. I tell you, Grover, it's been all I can do stopping him from killing you here and now.'

He looked towards the farm traffic passing along the drag at the end of the alley. 'Time to be on your way. I'll stay here out of sight. My face is on too many wanted posters for me to flaunt it in public unnecessarily.'

The line in the bank wasn't very long. Grover Lang looked at the clock over the vault door behind the teller. He was suddenly conscious of time as he watched the hand clunk to its next position, marking another minute during which his precious Little Jimmy was in the hands of violent strangers. Not to mention the spot Juanita was in.

'Good morning, Mr Lang,' the teller said as the old lady before him concluded her business and moved away from the counter.

The official's eyes caught Lang as he wiped perspiration from his forehead.

'Yes, it is a warm day, sir.'

'Yes,' Lang said. But it wasn't only the heat that was causing the dampness on his brow.

He took out his passbook and made his request to withdraw all his money.

'That's a considerable sum, Mr Lang,' the teller said as he compared the passbook with his ledger. 'Over fifteen thousand dollars.'

'I know.'

'And most unusual. Excuse me, while I speak with

the manager.'

Lang panicked and threw a glance at his escort who was standing glowering at his side. Paterson's hand moved down to rest on the belt near his gun and he looked across at the armed bank guard seated in a corner.

Seconds later the manager appeared. 'The teller has told me of your request. The fact is, to withdraw the complete sum means, effectively, that you will be closing the account. It is more usual to retain a deposit to keep the account open.'

Lang sighed in relief, realizing there was no significant problem. It was simply that the manager had an eye on future business.

'Why, of course. I suppose I could withdraw the straight fifteen thousand and leave the remainder.' He looked at Paterson, who nodded.

'That will be in order, Mr Lang,' the manager said. 'A bank draft will be acceptable, I presume?'

Lang not only caught the shake of Paterson's head but also the scowl that suddenly stretched his features.

'I require cash,' Lang explained. 'It's a condition of the business deal I'm involved in.'

'Now that presents a problem. We don't hold that much. We could arrange it for tomorrow, say.'

Lang's heart beat faster again and he didn't have to check Paterson's reaction.

'It must be today,' he said, his voice tightening.

'I see. Would you like to take a seat? I will need to make an arrangement with another bank in town for a loan. Just a formality, you understand. We give them a promissory note for the cash we need to make up the amount you require.'

'How long?'

'A quarter of an hour should do it.'

Lang watched the clock, heard its magnified ticking and hoped that the incongruous sight of himself, clean and well-dressed, sitting silently alongside an unshaven lump of scruff and trail-dust wouldn't arouse suspicion. He smiled weakly on the periodic occasions that the bank guard looked their way.

His mind was in turmoil. Once they'd got their hands on the cash what was stopping Crawford and his big bozo disposing of him in some way and simply vamoosing? Until they killed him, they would see him as a hazard in that he could engage the law.

He wiped his brow, looked at the clock and smiled yet again at the guard, praying the man would not suspect the odd-looking couple. It was in fact less than fifteen minutes but it seemed as though an hour had dragged by when the manager suddenly appeared behind the counter. The man's beaming face told him everything was all right. So far.

'What took so long?' Crawford asked when they were back in the alley. 'I thought there was trouble.'

'No sweat, boss,' Paterson said. 'You know how penpushers can drag their feet.'

Crawford opened the package and flipped the bills. 'How much?'

'Fifteen grand, boss.'

Crawford nodded in satisfaction, rewrapping the parcel. 'OK. We'll divvy up at the house. We got horses tied at the back of the alley. Grover can double up with me nice and cosy,' he said, adding in a sardonic tone, 'on account of it being we're pals.'

19

As they passed a stump that marked the entrance to his property Lang could see a buggy and couple of tethered horses outside the house he had called Moonbeam. The name now had a hollow ring. As they came closer he could see that the door had been busted open. They passed a stream and came to rest near a gentle hollow to the side of the veranda.

'The kid's in there,' Crawford said.

Lang's feet were first to hit the sand but Crawford stayed him from proceeding any further. 'Best I go first or you might get your head blown off.'

'Hey, Ed!' he shouted. 'It's me, Monte.' He mounted the veranda as the angled door creaked completely open.

The scarfaced man who appeared checked the visitors and sheathed his gun. 'You got the cash?' Ed asked.

As soon as Crawford said, 'No trouble,' Lang rushed past him and threw his arms round the tear-stained child within. 'It's OK, Jimmy. Uncle Grover's here now.'

'Now you've had your reunion,' Crawford said, slinging his saddle-bag on to a table, 'stay out of the way and don't cause any trouble.'

Before an eager audience he divided the money into three shares and handed each one over.

'Nothing to hang around here for any more,' he said as his comrades stashed their takes into their saddle-bags. 'Time to eat some trail dust.'

First at the doorway, he paused. 'It's gonna take you some time to get back, Grover, and when you do we'll be long gone. But if you get in touch with the law and anything happens to us as a result – any time, now or in the future – remember, we got contacts and we repay our debts. Even in prison there are ways of getting repayments from those who think they're safe and cosy on the outside. I'm sure you don't want anything to happen to the kid or his ma, so do yourself a favour, don't tell any authorities.' His lips stretched in a mocking smile. 'In the circumstances I don't think we'll exchange fond farewells.'

With that he touched his hat and the band moved into the sunlight.

But Paterson lingered in the doorway. 'You two saddle up,' he said. 'I'll be with you a minute. I got some unfinished business here.'

Crawford was already moving towards his horse when he heard the comment. He froze for a second while it sank in. 'No, Matt!'

He rushed back in to see Paterson's gun already lined up on Lang.

'No, there's no need.' Crawford said in a placatory tone. 'We've got the money. That's what all this was about.'

'Don't interfere, Monte, or I'll do for you too,' Paterson said, moving to one side so that his drawn gun could also partly cover his boss.

The gang leader looked at the threatening barrel. 'This is new, Matt. You've never threatened me before.'

'There was no call before.'

'You're gonna mess all this up, Matt.'

'Now, you step away from the kid,' Paterson snarled at Lang, motioning with his gun. 'I don't want to catch the little bugger with a slug. I got better plans for him. I'm gonna make him cry over his pa like ma cried over Nathan and Case.'

'I told you,' Crawford said, his voice increasing in firmness. 'He didn't kill them.'

'Hell, somebody's gonna pay and this critter fits the bill more than anybody.'

'Leave him to it, Monte,' the scarfaced Ed said, keeping his distance in the doorway.

Crawford paused for one more moment, then his

gun was out and spurting flame. Paterson turned and looked in amazement at his boss, before collapsing on the boards.

The gang boss checked that his shot had been fatal before retrieving Paterson's saddle-bag and helping himself to the man's cut.

'You didn't have to kill him, Monte,' Ed said.

'Yes I did. Once he showed he was set to mess things up he had to go. Just winging him would be no good. We got some trail to put behind us and a wounded man would hold us back.'

'And who gets that?' Ed said, gesturing to the dead man's money.

'We split it.'

'Hell, that's seven and a half grand each!' The scarfaced man pondered. 'Two and a half grand more. Jeez, that was two and a half grand for just one second's work with a bullet there.'

'I can do the calculations,' Crawford said, making for the door. 'Come on. We gotta make ourselves scarce.'

Ed picked up his own saddle-bag and hesitated, suddenly deep in thought. Only then did he walk slowly after the leader on to the veranda.

'Strikes me if you can do that to Matt, I reckon I gotta watch my own back, ain't I, Monte?'

'Don't be stupid, Ed. Come on.'

The man remained immobile. 'And just another second's work with a bullet could get you the whole caboodle, couldn't it, Monte?' There was a break as his mind continued to churn things over. 'Or me?'

The tone of his voice had changed and Crawford paused near his horse. 'Don't even think of it,' he said, his back to his colleague.

There was a momentary freezing of time and then the gang leader dived to one side. The two guns exploded simultaneously but Crawford's, even though fired from the ground, was the only one to hit its target.

Jimmy screamed and Lang appeared in the doorway, saw another new corpse. Saw Crawford pick up the dead man's saddle-bag and ease out the money.

The older man stepped down on to the sand to watch his one-time pal move across to scat the horses, then stride towards his own mount. Little Jimmy, face ashen and cheeks wet with fresh crying, joined his uncle and gripped his leg.

Lang moved a few more paces forward and stopped not far from the slight depression before the veranda.

Lots of things were going through his mind. All that had happened. And all that could happen.

Suddenly he cupped an arm round Jimmy, ran to the side with his precious bundle and rolled him down the slope. Crawford heard the noise and turned in time to see Lang sprinting back across the front of the house. He saw the older man making for the fallen form of the gang leader's latest casualty.

'What the hell you doing, Grover?' he yelled.

The older man dropped to the ground and came up with Ed's revolver in his hand.

Crawford laughed. 'You too? And what you gonna do?'

Lang raised the gun.

'Grover, you're a bridge engineer and a gold digger but you ain't no gun artist.'

'But I got the drop on you, Monte. That's the difference.'

Crawford laughed. 'Be sensible, Grover. You've just seen what I can do against a drawn gun – twice!'

The barrel remained levelled at Crawford's chest.

Whether it was Jimmy suddenly shouting out and momentarily drawing his attention, or whether Crawford had been right about Lang's lack of pistol skill, even when all the odds were lined in his favour would never be known, but he lost the advantage. Before he knew it Crawford's gun was out and being triggered. And Lang's own shot went predictably wide while the bullet from Crawford's gun took the skin off Lang's hand. The older man grunted and dropped the weapon, bending double as he gripped the wound.

At the sight of blood on his uncle Jimmy started crying again.

'Stay back, Jimmy!' Lang shouted.

Crawford slipped his own gun back into its holster. 'Sorry about that, Grover, but you asked for it. I did warn you. So be sensible. Pay heed to the kid. No need to distress him any more.'

He pointed at the bloodied hand. 'And see the problem you've got for yourself now? You just keep making things worse. Now, with that wound you're gonna have your work cut out getting the little mite back to his momma.'

He waggled his finger disapprovingly. 'Fact is, if you don't make it back with him, it'll be on your head.'

Lang glowered at him.

'Recognize when you're beat,' Crawford said and hauled himself up into the saddle. He gigged his horse and headed out. Knowing the older man was no good with a gun, especially now that his gun hand was a bloody mess, he didn't look back.

Lang lurched over to the stricken Jimmy and ran his hand over his head. 'Don't worry, kid, your old uncle's OK.' He threw a glance at Ed's horse, which had returned and to come to halt near the veranda, then he squinted at Crawford's receding figure.

His voice was firm when he whispered, 'Stay here, Jimmy.'

He tottered over to the animal and pulled the Winchester from its saddle boot.

'Keep back, kid,' he said as he stepped clear and

dropped to one knee. He laid the gun across his right forearm and awkwardly levered it with his left hand.

However his right arm itself had weakened with the effects of shock on his muscles so that he had difficulty raising the gun. Then, when he lined up, the pain shooting up from his hand caused the lower arm to quiver so it could not provide steady support.

A few steps ahead a low rock jutted from the ground. He dropped down behind it and used it to support the barrel. Once more he lined up and looked along the barrel. Resting on the hard rock, the gun was now steady. But the figure was a rapidly shrinking target and sweat was clouding Lang's vision. He lowered the gun and awkwardly wiped the sleeve of his left arm across his eyes and brow. Yet again he tried to aim.

Hell of a distance now, but nothing for it but to pull the trigger.

He worked his finger and there was an explosion.

But there was no reaction in the target. He cursed, knowing that given his clumsiness, by the time he relevered the gun for another shot it would be useless. Crawford would be an unattainable target.

But wait – Crawford was swaying in the saddle!

Lang stared unbelievingly as the man then slumped to the ground.

He took the opportunity to relever. He glanced to check that Jimmy was still out of harm's way, then loped as quickly as he could towards the fallen rider.

As Lang approached, he could see the back of the man's shirt staining fast. By the time he had got close up, Crawford had turned over. The bloody froth coming from the grimacing lips told Lang the bullet had hit a lung.

'That was unexpected,' Crawford croaked. 'Didn't know you could do it.'

'You were right back there,' Lang said. 'I don't have any experience with a handgun. But as a youngster I was in the college rifle team. Even earned myself a box of cigars once.'

Crawford coughed obscenely. 'Well, you've got more than cigars this time, pardner. I'm a goner, ain't I?'

Lang noted the swelling red stain on the front of the man's shirt indicating the bullet had gone right through. 'Reckon so.'

'Never thought you'd shoot your old pal.'

'Fact is, ain't seen you as a pal for a long time, Monte.'

'In the back yet.'

'But it still wasn't an easy decision to pull the trigger, especially that way. And I ain't proud of the backshooting.'

'You know, I saved your life once,' Crawford said, a hint of indignation in his weak voice.

'Yeah, and I've paid for it several times over.'

'Still . . . still. . . .'

'Still – nothing. Knowing you, the odds were you would be back when you'd blown the money. With the kid to look after I couldn't chance that.'

There was a pause before Crawford whispered, 'We had some good times, didn't we?'

'Reckon we did. . . .'

Lang didn't finish. Crawford's head had slumped to one side. He felt for a pulse and knew there was no point in continuing the sentence.

He walked over to the dead man's horse and extracted the money parcel from the saddle-bag.

Back at the house he comforted Jimmy, then washed his wound at the stream and bound it with a bandanna.

With one hand it would be a struggle travelling with the child but he could do it. As soon as he made Dana City he would telegraph the law office in Apache Flats and tell them to get over to his apartment pronto to release Juanita.

The sun shone strong over Apache Flats as the couple came out of the church. Little Jimmy was at their side dressed in a grand page costume, and two Mexicans were in the crowd throwing confetti over them.

It was six months later, the new house was completed, ready and waiting, and his hand had healed.

The sun was also shining once again on his life. There was no sign yet that the mine's riches were declining. He knew that the lode would not last forever but, when it did run out, he had already accumulated enough funds to make something of himself in town, maybe setting up some kind of business.

And enough funds to see him and his new family through some years to come.

With no looming shadow from his past like Monte Crawford to interfere.